PRAISE FO

&

BY THE TIME WE LEAVE HERE, WE'LL BE FRIENDS

"BY THE TIME WE LEAVE HERE, WE'LL BE FRIENDS is a David Lynchian nightmare set in a Russian gulag, where its prisoners, guards, traitors, soldiers, lovers, and demons fight for survival and their own rapidly deteriorating humanity. Osborne's debut novella is paranoid, cold, brutal, haunting, mystifying (in a good way), and totally unforgettable."
—Paul Tremblay, author of *The Little Sleep*

"The only thing crueler and weirder than life in Osborne's Stalinist gulag is the afterlife. Wringing an ergot-laced harvest of agony and absurdity from the bleak Siberian tundra, BY THE TIME WE LEAVE HERE, WE'LL BE FRIENDS manages the nigh-impossible feat of making Kafka's Penal Colony look like a Sweet Valley High romance."
—Cody Goodfellow, author of *Perfect Union*

"BY THE TIME WE LEAVE HERE, WE'LL BE FRIENDS is an opium-laced fever dream, swinging readily between the surreal and the horrifyingly, starkly real. Siberia is a place, metaphoric and literal: It's an inescapable, brutal state of mind. Give in to the voices and let this story deliver its kaleidoscopic nightmare, sly lines, and the truth of a bloody, damaged, beating, human heart."
—Monica Drake, author of *Clown Girl*

"Like a rat in a bag of deer meat—this is BY THE TIME WE LEAVE talking—Osborne's novella scuttles around inside you as you read it, and you come to know that rat as your own heart. And it knows you back, has all along."
    —Stephen Graham Jones, author of *It Came from Del Rio*

"This lyrical spatter of inspired dementia (as much a long poem as it is a novella) reminds me of Celine in serious nightmare mode, and yet its brutality is quiet—gentle even. To find yourself enjoying forensic black humor scenes of disgust and revulsion is a tribute to Osborne's writing—but also the deeper point I think he seeks to make.

We spend a great deal of time as a civilization earnestly wringing our hands and wondering how the all-too-real horrors of imprisonment, torture, and murder actually come to pass. Osborne's answer is alarmingly simple. They become not only possible, but indeed inevitable, not through perversion, but inversion. A crisis in the imagination makes the abnormal normal, even mundane, and the hideous matter of fact. War and prison aren't the causes of this calamity, they're logical expressions of it—and the potential for the schizoid crisis is with us all time. What is humiliation and destruction but compassion and creativity inverted? This happens first neither in prison camps nor stories about prison camps, but in the imagination and the human heart. And as Osborne reminds us—it happens easily. And it can happen to you.

Where in fact did the idea of prison camps emerge if not first in the imagination? Where will the cure for the human disease be found?"
    —Kris Saknussemm, author of *Private Midnight*

BY THE TIME WE LEAVE HERE, WE'LL BE FRIENDS

J. David Osborne

Swallowdown Press
Portland, OR

Swallowdown Press
PO Box 86810
Portland, OR 97286-0810

WWW.SWALLOWDOWNPRESS.COM

ISBN: 1-933929-05-7

Copyright ©2010 Swallowdown Press

By the Time We Leave Here, We'll Be Friends Copyright ©2010 by
James David Osborne

Cover art Copyright ©2010 by Alex Pardee

Interior art Copyright ©2010 by Erin Elise

Erin Elise photo Copyright ©2010 by Grace Fallen

Book design by Carlton Mellick III.

Printed in the USA.

For Andrew.

With thanks to Stacey Rios, Rob Vollmar,
Eric Brown, Samantha Doan, and Mike Carey.

Note on Use of Russian Language

Any Russian words which do not have commonplace modern English usage will first appear in *italics*, and then in standard typeface during any further appearances.

Though most words may be defined in context, a very short glossary follows for items which may not have follow-up English definition:

Chifir- Strong Russian tea with a mild psychoactive effect

Pridurok- Within the gulag, a prisoner treated as camp service personnel

Suka- Vulgar term of derision, similar to bitch, carries traitorous connotations

Urki- Common criminal

Ushanka- A heavy Russian fur cap

Valenkis- Russian winter boots

Vory v Zakone/Vor- "Thieves in law," the elite of the Russian world of organized crime, ruled the criminal underworld within the prison camps

Zek- Prisoner

"We Russians don't need to eat; we eat one another and this satisfies us."
—Anonymous,
from *Pushkin's Children*
by Tatyana Tolstaya

Quotas

The snow creaked like cartilage under their boots. The victims wore mottled black rubber welded together from scraps of flat tires. The lieutenant wore *valenkis* that shined, even in the lamplight.

The lieutenant nodded to the sentry and his German Shepherd on the way out of camp. The old man looked at the procession with sad eyes.

The prisoners paraded behind the lieutenant, left hands on the shoulders of the man in front. None of them protested.

When the camp was far enough away, he told them to get on their knees. Their faces were covered in Swiss-cheese burlap. Brown bloodstains.

He shot the first two without ceremony, exhaling with each shot, the bags puffing and steaming with cordite.

He fucked up the third, blew off the side of the man's face. Heard tooth fragments spear the snow. The victim began to spasm and cry. He scratched his cheek with his thumb, took a deep breath, and corrected his mistake.

The fourth caught his breath and said, "Do me a favor, and—"

Ilya Bogrov shot him cleanly in the top of the head.

He yanked off the holey burlap hoods. He squeezed them out and folded them and shoved them in his satchel. He squatted over the first body. Probed sticky gums with the fingers of his left hand, turning the dead men's grimaces into dog snarls, until the lantern picked up a glint of gold.

He sawed into the gums with his pocket knife. Worked a tooth back and forth until it snapped loose. He dropped the prize in his breast pocket and wiped his fingers on the corpse. There wasn't much blood in the mouth, but there was enough to make finding any more gold teeth a pain in his ass. He found gold in the next two mouths and moved to the final body.

The impact of the bullet had snapped the prisoner's head forward so sharply that he'd almost somersaulted. He lay in the snow, his shirt blood-stained and open. Bogrov did not take a tooth, but he leaned down with his pocket knife reaching just the same.

The Painter woke from his sleep to see Ilya Bogrov standing over him. He kicked at his sheets and grabbed at the walls, dream panic in his eyes, and Bogrov made no motion to stop him. Instead, he turned around and pushed the Painter's tool cart into a corner. The cart struck the wall and shiny tools jangled to the floor. The scared man caught his breath.

Bogrov sat in the chair next to the bed and took off his hat. His thin hair reached toward the sky in praise. He spread his legs and sat his cap on his knee.

The Painter shivered and covered himself with his blanket. "Appointment?"

"No."

"That's not mine," nodding at Bogrov's face.

Bogrov looked up, as if he'd forgotten it was there. The tattoo grinned above and between his eyes, a ghostly chakra. "No," he said. "Maybe before you were born."

"I was born a long time ago."

"Well," Ilya said. "Good."

The two men stared at each other for a long time.

Bogrov broke the silence. "Are you the only tattooist in camp?"

"As of a few months ago."

"What happened?"

"His sentence was up. He got to go home." The Painter laughed. Ilya Bogrov did not.

The small man's laugh choked off and he tried to swallow. Bogrov stood from the chair and replaced his cap and turned to go. He stopped at the door and tapped anxiously at the frame. Tapping. Thinking. He sighed and turned around. He reached into his pocket and removed a scrap of flesh that he'd cut from the last prisoner. A crude image of Lenin was scrawled amidst the curly hairs. He held it up to the Painter, whose eyes flashed with surprise, maybe recognition, then turned quickly to fear as Bogrov landed a wicked right cross that brought stars.

The Painter felt his mouth being wrenched open, felt the still-soft flesh crammed in, felt himself gagging. Then came the loudest pop he'd ever heard. He saw the soft gray of death for a few seconds, then saw nothing, ever again.

Apraxin hunched over his desk. The rhinoceros inkwell to his right danced with the quaking desk, desperate to please, but Apraxin was insatiable. His face was red and his fingers were stained black.

Bogrov stood at attention in front of him. Apraxin didn't look up, kept writing, until he was at the very end of the page. He stabbed the pen down and blew on the paper. Flipped into his outbox and folded his hands and took note of the soldier in front of him.

"Once I get going, you understand."

"Yes, sir."

"Can't stop or you lose that train of thought."

"Of course, sir."

Apraxin's fingers bloomed and he motioned for Bogrov to sit. "Is it done?"

"They are piled about a mile outside of town. I have Kopul burying them, now."

"And your report?"

Bogrov leaned to his left, creaking leather, and swiped a sheaf of papers from his satchel. "Four escapees this month, sir."

"It'll satisfy them."

"I hope so, sir."

Apraxin studied the report. He flipped a page, flipped back for a second, mouth moving with the words on the page. Bogrov fidgeted. The baroque furniture pressed the space around him. An empty picture frame lay face up on the desk. Apraxin set his report down. "Soldier, you half-assed it."

"Sir?"

"Why did these four men want to escape?"

"I don't know, sir."

"I know you don't know. But *they* need to know. They want to know that these men hated Mother Russia and all she stands for. You haven't made them villains here."

"I deeply apologize, sir."

"Don't apologize, just revise it. On second thought, I'll revise it, thank you."

Bogrov flushed. "Sir, I must insist."

Apraxin waved his hand. "Don't worry about it. You've done your part."

"Hardly, sir."

"You are dismissed."

Bogrov lingered for a moment. He scratched his cheek. Cleared his throat. The glossy painting of Stalin winked at him from over the fireplace. "Next time, sir, it will be perfect."

Apraxin looked up from his report. The silence was heavy. After a moment, Apraxin nodded. "...Alright. Thank you, lieutenant. Dismissed."

The soldier shot up like a rocket, saluted, and snapped to the door. Apraxin watched him leave.

The night air froze Bogrov's blood. He squinted into the snowfall and ground his teeth. He took off his gloves and plunged his hands into the snow and left them there until they turned blue.

Insomniacs

Alek Karriker was asleep for about an hour when the scar started to pulse, the skin around it glowing like he swallowed a flashlight. His jaw clenched against the paroxysms; he balled his fists and broke into a cold sweat. Then the scar on his neck separated, bloodlessly, from right to left. Light emanated from the cut, so bright it took on a solid tone, like a pearl, and it was from this blinding beam that Karriker's throat, wet and flapping, emerged, like a charmed snake, turning in slow counterclockwise circles, giving off a meditative hum that raised every hair on his body toward the ceiling.

After a few minutes the light shut off and his throat sucked back in like a tape measure and he was awake, no interim, no floating to the surface, none of those harrowing moments when dream threatens to become reality. No ceremony. Just awake.

He coughed. He hacked up a storm.

The room was pitch dark and *cold*. Siberian wind howled outside, tiny imperfections in the schoolhouse's framework sucking out what little heat the furnace—sitting in the corner with a dog-that-pissed-the-floor look on its face—was able to produce the night before.

Wiped crust from his eye. Clocked his sleep at two hours.

Massaged his throat. Felt like he'd swallowed a baseball.

Breathing in cliff-diver courage, he threw off his blanket and in one motion was on his feet. The frigid air showed no mercy. Tattooed skin popped gooseflesh, stretched tight over angry, angular bones. Blood rushed to his head. Massaged

14

his jaw. Teeth hurt.

Heat.

Flexed his fingers and danced on the tip of his toes to get his circulation going. He opened the furnace grate and swept out the ash pit with his hands.

Paper.

Grabbed an old *Pravda,* rolled up and neglected under his end table, wadded it up and spread it over the furnace grates. Spread an armful of kindling crossways and opened the flue.

Matches.

He spun to his room. Gun on the floor where he left it. Clothes scattered bachelor-style across the immense expanse of the room, coat draped over his chair, his pants like a closed accordion on the floor. The matches were alone in his pockets. He lit one and started the fire.

He threw on his overcoat and sheepskin *ushanka* and squatted close to the furnace, until sweat dripped down his face, and then he turned and warmed the base of his skull.

He used another match to light his lantern. The glow calmed him at first, but it soon took on a pulsing quality and he could hear his heartbeat, and he shook so hard that he stumbled to the corner where he kept his piss pot, and vomited.

Pain in his throat made him see stars.

Powder.

Karriker ripped the *Pravda* to an appropriately sized square and pinched black *makhorka* tobacco from the breast pocket of his coat and sprinkled it on the paper. From the inside pocket came a colorful bag, a gift from an Ngansan shaman. He poured opium into his tobacco like snow on a pile of manure. He rolled the cigarette and put it in his mouth and took a log out of the fire and let the flame lick at the end. He tasted the tobacco, and after a few moments the opium vaporized. He set the log back in the fire and breathed in the sweetness. Watched the blue smoke float through the weak red furnace glow.

His skin felt thick. His muscles loosened and he set the cigarette on the edge of his end table.

A cloudy chalkboard took up a good portion of the north wall, but it wasn't enough. The writing knew no bounds. It spilled passed the wooden borders onto the wall, down to the floor, up the bedposts and across the ceiling.

Karriker plucked the opium cigarette from between his lips and rolled off his cot. He shuffled across the expanse of the room, waving at the chalk dust he kicked up. He centered himself in front of the board and squinted at the centermost line of writing scratched across it. He followed the scrawl outward from there, followed as it spiraled and zigzagged and dropped off. None of it was in Russian. When the opium ran out he was standing on his bed, straining to look at the symbols chalked into the rafters.

He tossed the roach and got dressed and grabbed his shoeshine brush from under the cot. He opened his door and chucked the puke in his piss pot into the frigid morning. Scooped some snow into the pot, shook it around, and dumped it again. He scrubbed it with the brush. He set the bucket down and moved around the side of his house to take a shit. The morning cold crept into his asshole. He groaned out a squirt of stomach acid and gave up. He felt like vomiting again. He said the words, told himself he wanted to die.

He buckled his belt and almost missed the white

graffiti plastered along the sides of the schoolhouse that, as best as he could make out, read, *suka*. The same way dogs sometimes turn expectantly at the sound of a curse, so did Karriker respond to suka. He heard it on his daily patrols, at his desk when he processed new inmates, sometimes when he was alone. He stared at the vandalism, slackjawed.

He nearly threw the door off its hinges. His breathing intensified but his eyes stayed dead and distant.

He scooped another bucket of snow from outside and set it on the stove and watched it melt. He dipped the shoe brush into the pail and cleaned the chalkboard from corner to corner. Mystical writing, gone. A sheen of deep green began to dilate as it dried. Then he went to work on the walls.

Opium's fingers smoothed the contours of his brain. He felt the rage leaking through his pores, crusting on his skin. He wiped a streak of chalk off his bedpost. The thought of open veins, tangles of nerve endings and meat. He dropped the brush into the white water and set it by the stove.

He turned to go to back to bed and found himself staring down the barrel of his own gun.

He was almost impressed at how silently the *zek* broke into his room. The prisoner was wild-eyed and chewing and panting. He gripped Karriker's carbine in his quivering dirt-crusted hands. Karriker closed his eyes and said. "I did what I thought was necessary."

The zek spoke calm, lightly accented Russian. "I'm not interested in what you've done. I'm interested in what you're *going* to do."

Karriker opened his eyes. "You're a long way from Poland."

The Pole had one eye squeezed shut and the other

bloodshot and staring down the barrel of the carbine. "Everyone's a long way from home, here."

Karriker said nothing.

The zek coughed and cleared his throat. "And some of us would like to see our homes again."

Karriker was quiet until it was clear he was meant to speak. "This is a poor way of going about it."

"Better than starving."

"It's *quicker* than starving."

The Pole stepped closer. "No threats, please."

"Okay, no threats." The only sound was the wind and the metronome of the intruder's chewing.

A hot orange itch razed the scar across Alek Karriker's neck and he lifted one hand out of the air to scratch and the zek stepped forward. "Hands up."

Alek listened and rolled his head around his shoulders, feebly trying to use the stubble on his chin to scratch. The zek peeled his cheek off the carbine and lowered it a hair. "What's wrong with you?"

"It's nothing." Alek shook his head and cleared his throat.

"Stop."

Karriker stopped.

"Do you know why I'm here?"

"Tely sent you?"

"Never heard of him."

"Oh." Karriker put his hands down. "In that case you must be hungry."

"Yes. Hands up."

Karriker walked toward his bed, using two fingers to point the barrel of the gun away from him. "Why didn't you just ask?"

"It's not that easy."

"It *is* that easy."

"I don't have anything to trade. As soon as I get something, those fucking savages steal it."

"I'm a charitable guy. I don't want to see anyone die."

"Yesterday, in the commons. I watched an old man die. He starved."

"I saw him, too. By the mess hall."

"You didn't help *him*."

Karriker lit a cigarette and leaned his elbows on his knees. He blew smoke out his nose and turned his palms up in a shrug. "He didn't come to me. Didn't ask."

"Just tell me where you hide it."

"No."

The Pole raised the weapon, chewing even louder.

"If they hear a gunshot, they'll be on you," Karriker clapped his hands, "like that. You'll never have your bread."

"Suka."

Karriker smiled. "I see you've seen the graffiti. I hope it wasn't you that painted it."

"No, it wasn't."

Big dragon exhale. "Good."

The prisoner sighed and hefted the carbine.

"Do it."

The Pole spit out a chunk of paraffin. It bounced once. "I'm just trying to get a fucking piece of bread."

"Indeed. Indeed." Karriker began scratching at a series of numbers chalked over his cot. "Ask me."

"Ask?"

Karriker studied the grit under his thumb. Spread his hands wide. "Ask and you shall receive."

The zek lowered the gun. "That's all I have to do?"

"I told you, I'm a charitable man. Just ask."

The zek looked at the ceiling and rubbed his forehead. "May I have a piece of bread?"

"May I have a piece of bread…"

"May I have a piece of bread, *please*?"

Karriker flicked his cigarette off of the Pole's chest. "Absolutely not. Get the fuck out of my house."

The smoke hung in the air. The zek coughed and wiped the ash off of his shirt, keeping the gun aimed at Karriker. The coughing mutated into a high pitched giggle, and soon the intruder was laughing hard, and Karriker couldn't help himself, he was laughing too. The zek began nodding, wiggling his eyebrows, saluting Karriker's sense of humor. Then he raised the rifle and pulled the trigger.

The gun clicked.

Karriker hopped off his bed and cheerfully plucked the carbine from the stunned prisoner, flipped it around, and planted the butt into his stomach. His air rushed out and he crumpled in a heap on the floor.

Karriker tossed the gun. "They don't give *priduroks* bullets. I don't know why." He sat on the bed and lit another cigarette. Waved out the match and tossed it, mock hard, in the zek's face. He studied the hot glowing end of his cigarette. "Most of us are nice people."

The Pole clenched his belly and tried to breathe.

"I've been a pridurok for a while. They gave me the uniform…must've been more than a year ago. Still, rules are rules. If you used to be *urki*, you can't shoot people. Which is fine by me." The prisoner was retching. Alek sighed. "Calm down. Focus on catching your breath."

The zek wheezed and bared his teeth.

"Camp's got two kinds of people. The ones focused on living, and the ones focused on killing." He kissed the crucifix around his neck. "Get up."

The prisoner climbed onto all fours.

"What's your name?"

The zek said "Hipolit" to the floor.

"Well, Hipolit, you owe me."

Hipolit stood up. His eyes drilled holes into Karriker.

Karriker stared down the length of his cigarette like a sniper. "You can leave."

The Pole looked at the door like a cliffs edge, but when he turned back he found no humor behind the curtain of tobacco smoke, so he stumbled for it, nursing cracked ribs, glancing back several times, waiting for the deadly rush of air that never came, and he pushed open the beaten door and disappeared.

Alek Karriker tip-toed to the door and peaked out and watched the zek enter his barracks. He closed the door.

Karriker kept his stash under the floorboards, under the bed. Fifteen black rocks of bread, three corked bottles of good vodka, one bottle of homemade, twelve packs of cigarettes, a small cylinder of streptomycin tabs, and an ounce of *chifir*. He took a bite of bread and crumbled the rest. He dumped the dirty chalk water and refilled the bucket with snow and set it on the stove and waited. He produced a mortar and pestle from under his bed and mixed water with the bread crumbs and ground until it was paste.

He huddled over a stack of camp stationary, a tangle of bone and sinew and cigarette smoke, cutting the paper into small strips with a scalpel.

He was patterned with a thick foliage of old tattoos.

21

Inked beetles skittered across geometric patterns in his hands. The knuckles of his left hand announced his name. A lightning-bolt cat drowned the entirety of his right forearm. The landscape of his back was an epic ziggurat mural, one spire for each year in prison. And across his chest, a royal flush, in spades.

Karriker dipped the strips of paper in the paste and layered them, four strips to one card.

He read a paperback copy of *Volokolamsk Highway* by Aleksandr Bek while he waited for the strips to dry. His eyes got tired and he set the book down and paced his room.

He took two streptomycin pills from his stash. He never used them for his tuberculosis. He crushed them and mixed them with water. When he was at the White Swan, he'd seen zeks try to use their blood for red. TB meds were vastly superior. The reds *popped*.

Karriker fired up a lighter and toasted a boot heel into soot.

He worked for a few hours, his hands moving freely, his mind taking the backseat. He put painstaking detail onto the nude women spread across his face cards and embellished the rest with flowers and skulls and cats. As he put the finishing touch on his deck of cards, he noticed that the chalk writing had returned to the board, and that it whispered to him, and every once in a while, his throat would heat up and whisper back.

Reveille

A monotonous sound, faint at first, of a hammer on metal. As the sound got closer it got clumsier, and soon it was like some drunk animal had gotten into camp, bleating and dying.

Alek Karriker got dressed. He hefted his carbine from its post near the door and stepped out into the cold. He tucked his chin to chest out of habit and let his body acclimate. The reveille was getting louder. The rows of wooden barracks stayed still, extinguished lanterns swinging from their doorframes. Ignoring as long as they could.

To the south the watchtowers panned a searchlight across the courtyard, plaid squares of light drifting back and forth through the gaps in the buildings, then dark. He snapped his chinstrap to keep the wind from blowing off his ushanka. It was so dark it felt like someone had replaced his eyes with hunks of coal. Felt like he'd be sick again but his stomach was empty. When the searchlight wandered past again a bright electric buzz filled his ears and he thought he'd collapse.

Lanterns lit along the rows of barracks. Doors opened. Whistles blew. Dogs barked.

It was time for the camp to wake up.

"You hear it. You know what time it is. Wake up."

Blankets rustled, feet kicked. Emaciated bodies scrambled to get on the floor, at attention. Karriker braced himself against the smell: skin and sweat and tooth rot.

23

The prisoners wore loose-fitting gray trousers with black numbers smudged across the breast and the same numbers, larger, across their back.

Karriker prowled the length of the room, zeks tumbling from the top bunks. Found Hipolit towards the back, sitting on his bed, kissing a glossy black and white photo of a lovely young woman. He couldn't be sure if the Pole was wiping dust from the picture or stroking the woman's face, but when he heard Karriker's boots on the floor he pocketed the picture and hopped to his feet. Karriker clapped him on the shoulder and nodded at his pocket. "How are your ribs?"

The zek's hands trembled. He clenched his jaw.

Karriker's voice got low. "You look tired."

"I feel fine."

Karriker pointed at the knife notches in Hipolit's bunk post. Doing his best at looking solemn: "Can seem like forever."

"It can." The zek blinked.

"My advice, you'll go crazy trying to count the days. Don't keep track. Let it blur." He counted the notches, mouthing the numbers. Shook his head. "Besides, you'll run out of space one of these days." He stared hard at the wiry prisoner. "You need anything, my friend?"

Realization flickered in the zek's eye like a muzzle flash. "No."

"Bread? Cigarettes?"

Hipolit shook his head, starting to sweat.

"Maybe a book? I've got plenty of books."

Hipolit opened a desert-dry mouth, face twitching under the stares of the needle-toothed criminals—yellow skinned and hissing and writhing around the barracks, watching and taking notes.

"If you need anything, my door is open." There was no sound in the barrack except for the rustle of clothing on skin. Hipolit had become a piece of meat.

Karriker's lips curled in the tiniest of smiles and he walked away, barking orders at the prisoners, and the spell was broken.

He exited the barracks certain he had filled Hipolit's veins with gasoline and left his heart sparking with the desire to run.

Some zeks joked quietly with each other as they dressed. Karriker listened to a man talk about his dream. He was born of a chicken and clawed his way from the egg. Poured his vital fluids into a skillet and ate them and grew feathers.

Most were silent, their eyes distant and dumb. They stared at the floor with the bewilderment of a student faced with a test he didn't study for. Karriker stalked the aisle, appraising the condition of the prisoners. A zek, mouth open like a screaming skull, had fallen asleep against his bed post, his arms slung up in a halfway pulled-on shirt. Karriker scooped the zek's boots up from the floor and carried them outside, where he dipped them into the snow. He let the boots fall at the foot of the man's bed, heavy, flakes spiraling onto the floor. The man didn't seem to notice, and when Karriker slapped him, he fell back onto the bed. Karriker placed his forefinger under the man's nose to be sure, then told everyone to clear out.

The zeks began to shuffle, a couple of them chewing the insides of their cheeks, keeping a vulture eye on the dead man's bunk on their way out. Once the room was empty,

Karriker rolled the corpse and tossed the mattress to the floor and ran his hand along the inside of the frame. It was unusual to find any kind of food, but occasionally there would be tobacco. No luck. He hooked his finger into the dead man's cheek and probed for gold. He undressed the body and threw the clothes in a heap by the door and dragged the body by its wrist out into the cold.

He hauled the corpse around the Sector A barracks, through the alley between the small armory and the brick hospital where the barbed wire gapped, and up the hill overlooking the camp. He dumped it in a shallow grave, where it landed face-up on another corpse already blue and covered in frost. Karriker cinched his jacket tighter and started down the hill.

At least the morning wasn't a complete waste: Karriker reached into his own pocket and unfolded the Pole's picture, the photo of the woman. It was strained—she was extremely posed, high cheekbones and heavy eyelids.

He tore the picture to shreds and headed for the courtyard.

Assignments

Zeks assembled for their daily assignments. Russians and Poles mostly, a few Turks, a few Americans, some Asiatics, could be Inuit, could be Chinese. They yawned and warmed their hands. A few stretched. They exchanged cigarettes and stared at the dawn. Their necks sunk into their shoulders. They kept one hand clenched around their trousers.

Transport trucks' ignitions grumbled, smoke roiling from their exhaust pipes.

The sun was trying to peek through the slate gray clouds and Karriker stopped and took in the scene and sighed.

That morning Apraxin wore a fine goat-skin *fufaika* and leather gloves. Always made Karriker laugh. On the inside. The great unwashed masses huddled together, a giant dark gray dust ball, listening carefully to the elocutions of the only man in camp with a record player.

"Barracks A-20 through A-35 will ship to Sector 6. Barracks B-1 through B-12 will ship to Sector 3," and on and on, his trim words swallowed up by the black hole in front of him. He went through the paces. Once he was done he tucked his clipboard under his arms and said, "Stay warm, men. Another glorious day to serve Mother Russia," and cleared his throat and gave a nod to the crowd and marched back to his office without a glance back.

Karriker worked the kinks out of his arms and waved zeks into the trucks, pointing with his right and wind-milling his left. They packed in shoulder to shoulder and Karriker closed the tailgates and gave the drivers a thumbs up.

He kept pace alongside the convoy, enjoying the

warm exhaust in his face. He nodded at a couple guards lounging in the sally port and they smoked and ignored him. The convoy disappeared around a bend in the woods and Karriker lit a cigarette and strolled along the barbed wire trenches. The wind felt him up, found all the cracks in his clothes and slipped in.

Anton Nikitin was where he always was, sitting on a scarred stool with a book in his lap, tired from a night of patrolling the camp's perimeter with his German shepherd, Tatyana. Karriker bummed a cigarette. Tatyana wagged her tail and he stroked her fur and the concentric circles of bare skin. Tatyana never seemed to mind being a canvas.

Nikitin folded his creaking arms and crossed his legs. "I don't understand how I can walk all night, until my feet are screaming, and then sit on this stool and not fifteen minutes go by before my ass hurts more than my feet."

"At least your shift is over."

"I'd rather be working." He stamped patterns into the snow with his boot. Tatyana's tail wagged, the design on her rump caterpillaring into a spiral. "Dogs are the perfect animal. She would rip your throat out if I asked her to." He clawed at her neck and her eyes narrowed with pleasure. "I'm convinced, though I'm no expert in biology, if you cut a dog's brain open it would just be a perfect little human brain, with none of the bad parts."

Karriker smoked and tried not to hold a single thought for too long. Tatyana stalked over to a spot a few yards away and began digging a hole in the permafrost.

Nikitin bit the dry skin from his lips. "Don't you have somewhere to be, boy?"

"No." He glanced down at the book Nikitin was holding in place with his finger. "What're you reading?"

BY THE TIME WE LEAVE HERE, WE'LL BE FRIENDS

Nikitin glanced at it like he'd forgotten it was there. "This?" He studied the spine. "*Vladimir Tyorkin.*"

Karriker recoiled. "Why?"

"Because it's good."

Karriker smoked. "Any book in which a man shoots down a plane with a rifle is bullshit."

Nikitin slid his finger from between the pages and slipped the book under his thigh. "Just because you haven't seen it done doesn't mean it hasn't been done."

"Tyorkin swims a freezing river to murder a platoon of Nazis with his bare hands. And when he's done, he swims back across the river to his camp and plays the accordion for his comrades."

Nikitin huffed and tugged the novel from under his leg. He tossed it on the ground. "No need to read it, now."

"Sorry. Just trying to prove a point."

Nikitin bunched his face up. "What's wrong with all that? It's inspirational."

Karriker smoked his cigarette for a moment. "Books like that turn Dostoevsky in his grave."

He was like an acupuncturist, knowing exactly which nerves to touch to elicit a reaction from the old man. Nikitin spit. "Dostoevsky was no good communist. Books full of pussies." The loose skin of his neck shook as he spoke. "If RAPP had had their way, it'd all be shit like that. Books for pussies. By pussies. To be Soviet is many things, pussy is not one of them. Us, of all people, should understand this. We see every day what the Soviet man can endure."

"In America, they have Superman. You know Superman?"

Nikitin flinched. "Yes."

"He's from another planet."

"Americans believe in nothing."

Tatyana dug. They watched for a while, then Karriker walked the old man back to his room. The younger man tried to ignore the cold, the aches in his bones. *Opium.* He talked to Nikitin outside his barracks.

Tatyana was already curled up by Nikitin's bed, chewing a bone. Karriker told him goodbye and started back. Smelled the trees. He watched a group of zeks repairing a collapsed barrack roof, snow tumbling off of it in sheets. Passed a group carrying pails of frozen water.

He needed another smoke.

Opium Dens

Karriker laid on his side. The midday sun was blocked by a strong velvet curtain. The sound of the paper unwrapping gave him chills. He held his pipe close.

The room was soft by camp standards. There were smooth edges and good smells and pillows on the cots. Color, too, cerise pillows inlaid with gold and creaseless purple blankets. Silk. Even the smells in the room were pleasant, black and green teas and rice boiling in the stove. And opium.

Wu lifted a metal poker and balanced it over a brass and paktong lamp. The end of the poker glowed a brilliant red and he stuck it into a crumbling pile of opium nestled in a ceramic dish.

The tiny man put the cold end of the poker between his knees and used his nails to mold the moist drug into a cone. He blew on it and removed it gingerly and dropped it in the doorknob bowl. He nodded and Karriker swiveled the pipe over the lamp's funnel top. Wu pursed his lips and lifted his upturned palms to the ceiling. The steam crawled from the edges of the bowl and Karriker pressed his lips to the pipe and the insides of his cheeks nearly touched as he inhaled the vaporized O.

Best thing he'd tasted in the past week. The candles inside the paper lamps blurred at the edges and he rubbed his palm along the plush cushion and tilted his head back and released the cold smoke into the air.

Wu took a seat behind his great mahogany desk with

31

the jade dragon statue and the bust of Stalin and adjusted his thick glasses and started writing. The sound of pen scratches went underwater, and soon Karriker was asleep.

In Karriker's dreams he felt like the sun was shining on his face.

Hipolit's Ear

Hipolit inhaled the dust. His face and clothes were black. He brought his pick down and squinted against the spark and dumped the rocks into the cart. The tires squeaked against the rails as the ore climbed to the surface.

He tried to breathe. The cart reached the surface, and when the break bell rang that day no one had died yet.

He shielded his eyes from the dying sun and collected his bread ration from the slit window in the mess hall, mixed it with water and swallowed quickly. He turned his back on the billowing purple sunset and opened the squeaky door to his barracks. He wormed his way through the after-work throngs and threw himself onto his cot and caught his breath and did his best to ignore the breathy masturbation of his bunkmates. They jerked off whenever they pleased, some of them talked casually while they did it.

His stomach was sore from his last ration of bread. His throat was dry and he could feel himself drifting into sleep. He fingered his pocket and felt nothing but the stitched lining.

Someone in the barracks laughed at a *vor* shooting a thick rope of semen onto the floor.

Panic set in.

He hopped up and shuffled the straw mattress off the frame, running his fingers into splinters along the posts. He peeled open the mattress and rooted, knowing that his picture wouldn't be in there.

A scabrous vor in the adjacent bunk hunched over his

33

boots, lacing them up and then unlacing them, batting at the strings like a cat, then lacing them again. Hipolit approached him slowly.

"Excuse me."

The vor didn't look up from what he was doing. He took the laces in either hand and dumped them in the boot, then shook it, rattling the plastic tips.

"Excuse me."

The vor picked up the boot and slammed it down, hard. Then did it again. Grunting.

Hipolit was about to open his mouth again when the gangster looked up at him. His head was shaved and ridged where a scar dug deep. Robin's eggs for eyes. He set the boot in his lap and chewed on the strings. Folded his arms, like he was listening.

"I'm looking for a picture."

The criminal tilted his head, offering up his ear. He started to suck the saliva that had sponged into the lace.

"It's a black and white picture of a woman."

The vor shook his head.

"No? You haven't?"

He tossed the boot aside and stood up. The moisture in his breath mutated to sweat that rolled off Hipolit's brow. The criminal clenched his fist and stuck out his thumb and touched it to each side of his neck, then patted on the center of Hipolit's forehead.

"You buy bread from that suka."

Hipolit couldn't swallow. "N-no." This was happening too fast. He should have known better. Something hard and sharp played along his inner thigh.

"Next time you see that suka."

"I don't."

"Next time, you see him." The vor gave him a look that said, 'Pay attention.' "Next time, you ask *him* where your picture is." He pressed the blade in just enough to draw blood, to make Hipolit gasp. "And then maybe you don't buy bread from him, no more. Yes?"

Hipolit went prone and caught his breath. He mashed his pant leg into the cut with his thumb.

The thief walked back to his boots and snaked the laces from inside and wrapped them around his hand and said, "The others are thinking of what to do with you."

The blood was making Hipolit sick. He tried to tear the bed sheet but couldn't, so he twisted the whole thing and wrapped it around his leg.

"That cut is not so big. You won't like more."

"No, I wouldn't."

"I am a man who likes to have fun."

Hipolit's eyes worked nervously. The room had started to magnetize, he could feel the hum, he could see the bodies turning, moving closer without lifting a foot.

"I am a man who likes to have fun more than he likes to kill bitches. But my friends, they want to kill you. Because you cannot be trading with the suka. His time is close, but your time doesn't have to be. Your time can be anywhere. Any time." He lifted up his shoelace. "You are going to have to earn it if you do not wish to die."

Blind Cow Eye

The opium high got deep into his soul. He talked and Wu listened, and soon the medicine man was nodding and stroking his beard and moving about the room, rummaging through shelves and uncorking bottles. He stood over him, seemingly huge in his zek uniform, and his lips moved, Karriker heard Oriental, then it got quieter and quieter and a couple seconds later the words came out, monotone Russian. The words did not match the lips. Wu extended a bony yellow claw, inch-long fingernails, clasping a bag. Karriker held his hand out. Wu pointed in his face.

"Mix with tobacco. Smoke as quickly as possible."

"What is this?"

"Blind eye of a cow."

"You want me to smoke cow eye."

"Blind cow eye."

"Where do you get this shit?"

"If you smoke too much, you'll go blind."

"Got it."

"So don't do it too much."

"Got it."

The night air froze his guts. Tasted cinnamon on his lips. Moved toward the pridurok barracks. The thieves. The gang members. Murderers. Rapists. His people. A chorus of off-key drunk voices in the dark.

Reaching into his breast pocket, he stuck the slender cow eye cigarette into his mouth and lit the tip. Sour liquid dripped out the back of the cig. Sucked his cheeks in and watched the glowing paper crack and spiral off into the night.

The effect was instant. The buildings' facades peeled back like turning pages. Zeks huddled by stoves. They played cards. A thief stared at scribbled paper. Karriker focused harder and the man's skin filleted away and Karriker could see his heart pulsing.

More to south, deeper into the thieves' quarters, the cow eye magic plucked the frame off the barracks like a sheet off a bird cage. He watched revelers imbibe their poisons, watched their esophagi pop and hiss from the vile toilet vodka. A few slept in corners, rosy cheeked, drool and vomit on their shirtfronts.

In the Sector A he saw Hipolit, the Pole, with his ear tied in a piece of string, looped like a bicycle chain around the ear of another zek. The Pole was crying and the zek was laughing, the bootstraps cutting into his ear.

In Barrack B-9 he watched a card game.

They were using his cards. Smoking. Drinking. Big pile of cigarettes in the center of the table. Cards thrown. Fingers pointed. Another drink poured.

Killing his buzz.

Inside his pocket watch he saw the wheels and cogs and pins clicking and spinning. Forty-five minutes passed. His mind stepped down from the higher plane. The barracks regained their skin, the wooden walls faded back into view.

Shower

A pair of bruised hands broke the water. Dust and dirt Van Goghed from calloused fingers till the water blackened to ink.

The zek let his hands sit like that for a minute or two and closed his eyes. The water stung the fresh cuts. He waited for the ripples to disappear, then he splashed his hands up quickly, smacking himself in the face with the water, and he picked up the black slug of soap from the table and dragged it across his yellow skin. He cupped his hand into the water again and patted down all the foamy streaks across his torso. He got under his arms and balls.

Hefting the entire washbasin above his head, he tilted it toward him and the water matted his beard and slicked back his hair, and he flung the water from his face and spit it from his mouth, and he looked over to where Ilya Bogrov sat nursing his carbine in the corner, and he held out his hand.

Bogrov reached under his stool, tossed him a towel.

"Thank you."

Bogrov picked up the carbine and laid it across his lap.

The prisoner dried furiously. He mussed his hair and beat the towel against his beard. When he was done he held it out to Bogrov, who pointed to the pile in the corner, next to the spigot.

"Of course," the prisoner said, smacking his head. Tossed the towel. He picked up his pants from where he'd dropped them and struggled in. "This what you do all day?"

Bogrov lit a cigarette.

"Watch men take baths?"

Bogrov held the smoke in.

The prisoner smiled, his cheeks getting a shade pink. "Boring job."

And he breathed it out. "You can go, now."

"You must have pissed somebody off."

Bogrov kept his jaw square. He scratched under his eye, or maybe he was brushing something off his cheek.

"Did you request this?"

Bogrov looked at the man for a long time. "It's just the job they gave me."

"Oh, I forgot." The man pulling on his parka. "They don't give you choices."

Bogrov shook his head.

The prisoner tossed Bogrov the soap. He dropped it in the empty wash bucket. The zek winked. "Learn to love it, I guess."

Ilya Bogrov finished his cigarette before calling in the next in line.

The Gun is Good

Karriker brushed snow off his uniform. A crumbled newspaper already crackled in the stove and he let his hands go from numb to stinging to warm. He peeled off his clothes and threw them in a heavy, sopping pile. He sat on his bed for a moment and picked up *Volokolamsk Highway* from his bedside table and fanned the pages and smelled the pulp. Picking his wet clothes up, he placed them onto the furnace and shuddered at the sizzle.

He kicked his feet up and laid back on the bed. Letters swam lazily through the soup of his mind, and he reached out like a child fumbling for a fish in a stream, and the letters scattered. A few came back to nibble at his fingers and these letters formed ideas.

He pressed his chin to his neck and stared across the room at his closet. It stared back at him. They stayed like that for a long time, until the closet began to float down an imaginary hallway, further and further away, but still front and center in his mind, impossibly big, every crack a trench where mud drenched men slept with one black hand clamped down on their helmets, dying in yellow clouds of gas.

The closet said, "You feel really good right now."

The doors swung open and lights illuminated plush silk lining, like the inside of a coffin, the inside of Lenin's coffin, encased in glass, and Karriker dropped his hand, his palm running along not splintered wood but smooth, polished oak, and instead of Lenin staring out at him he's staring down the barrel of a machine gun, a giant Gatling gun, and it all made sense: *your closet is where you keep your gun, and it is good.* He reached out to touch the gargantuan thing and instead felt the stomach of a dragon taking up the entire sky, shrouding the sun and digesting the moon, the mouth somewhere else, hungry, ready to swallow the world whole.

He rapped his knuckles against his skull and perked up.

Sober up. Options rolled through his mind. *Cigarette.*

He dressed in dry clothes and clicked the closet shut and warmed his palms by the furnace and rubbed his face.

Karriker blew into his hands and stepped out of his front door, almost knocking into the two giant reindeer melting the snow in front of him.

He backpedaled and tripped on his doorstep and landed flat on his ass. His big gloved fingers fumbled for his carbine, and when he got hold of it he swung it like a club, knocking a hole in the bigger deer's neck, but the beast didn't move and the wound did not yield blood. The other deer didn't run off or come to her friend's rescue. Neither of the animals flinched.

Karriker gasped and tasted the opium and cow eye, he saw himself and the scene on a dark stage, the audience hushed, the snow melting on his coat. The lights went up, there was no audience, just an empty auditorium, red fold down seats empty except for ghosts, and in the middle of the middle row, the largest man Karriker had ever seen hopped from his seat and made his way to the aisle, the ghosts pulling in their legs and pretending that it's no big deal and cursing him under their breath. His hair was white and wild and he was adorned in bright pink tattoos. He hoisted himself onto the stage, the snow (actually not snow, but sodium polyacrylate, mixed in a giant plastic

bowl that morning by, Karriker guessed, the same genius
that stuffed these two reindeer) floating off the stage in
lazy clouds. The giant pulled what Karriker thought was
a rolled up *Pravda*, but instead he unrolled the paper
and attempted to bend back the curled edges. He leafed
through the pages, stapled together in the upper-left-hand
corner, until he got to a page near the end. He creased
the corner and pointed a dirty fingernail at a line in the
middle of the page:

ALEK KARRIKER falls to the ground.
He glances to his left and right.
Unable to discern who might have done this,
he says, incredulously,

ALEK KARRIKER:
What the fuck?

The giant, who was obviously the director, took out a
red marker and underlined "incredulously" and said, "You
haven't said your line and already I do not believe you are
incredulous enough." His teeth filed to points.

Everything disappeared, the giant, the stage, the chairs,
everything except for the two stoic reindeer, mocking him
with their permanence. Karriker stood up and brushed the
snow off his coat and let his eyes readjust themselves.

Karriker nudged the deer with the butt of his rifle.
Nothing. No blinks, no subtle heaving of lungs, no tensing
of muscles. Dead. Stuffed.

The animals were warm, and as he stepped in closer to
investigate he realized that they'd turned the snow under
them into a muddy puddle. He touched the slight fur of

the beast and the warmth shot up his arm and soon his whole body was warm. He slowly wrapped both arms around the deer on his right and hugged it for a long time. When he stepped back he was red and the cold was that much worse.

Both reindeer were slit open from the crotch to the breast. Their bellies were soft, thinly haired and pocked with warts. Karriker slid his hands into where their guts should have been and felt around. Extremely warm, but empty. Smelled like sweat.

He forced his arm in, getting elbow deep, grasping for anything. He could feel a frustrated howl gestating in his stomach, but he kept it inside. Sweat was breaking out on his face and he wondered how a dead thing could be so warm. Soon his fingers closed around something wet. He pulled it out and shook the blood off. It was purple, blue and red, the size of a dinner plate, covered with veins. Afterbirth.

Karriker said, mostly to himself, "What the fuck?"

He walked around the reindeer a few times, not sure what to do. The sky was still pitch black that night and there was no reveille. He wasn't sure if anyone had seen him. He walked to the east end of the barracks and looked around the corner. Empty. He checked the west end, which was also empty both ways. The placenta sagged in his palm.

He stepped into his room: bed, clothes on the furnace, closet, desk, scattered pens. He checked under the bed, in the closet. His head was the head of a pin in a ball room, sticking straight into the floor as dancers swirled around him. Waves of nausea.

When he went outside again, the deer were gone.

Hunt

After seeing the prisoners off, Karriker wandered to the camp's entrance, staring at a reindeer, running at full speed and a bug's crawl, at the same time, in the creases of his palm. Karriker blinked and shook his head and said, "Nikitin."

"What?"

"Are there lots of reindeer around this area at this time of year?"

Nikitin smoked. "Yes. Want to shoot some?"

Karriker scratched Tatyana behind the ear. "Yes." The dog rested her head on Karriker's thigh. Her paws were caked in mud; the hole she was digging was getting sizable. He rubbed her head. "What do you think she's digging up?"

"I don't know. Maybe bodies."

"Could be."

"Could be something else."

They stared at the hole. Karriker said, "Probably bodies."

Nikitin nodded. "Probably."

Tatyana caught the scent, Nikitin took the shot, and Karriker got to it first. The reindeer splayed out in the snow, blood tumbling from its neck, and he ran his dagger from its breast bone to its belly and its fat tongue rolled around in its snout and its hot guts poisoned the snow. Karriker parted the wound with his fingers and stuck his full fist in.

Nikitin caught his breath, and Tatyana tilted her head and both of them stared at Karriker as he held up one blood-soaked fist and smiled and said, "Everything's there. Everything is good. Everything is there."

Back at camp, Nikitin had put his ushanka on. He was smoking a cigarette and it took him a second to get the pack out of his jacket to offer one to Karriker. Karriker brushed dried blood off his cheek and picked out a smoke.

Nikitin pushed the sack full of deer meat behind his chair and rummaged through his satchel. Took out a paperback.

Karriker held out his hand. "What're you reading?"

Nikitin checked the spine like he always did. "Eh... *Locusts* by Sergei Budantsev."

"What's it about?"

"Locusts."

"A novel?"

"Yes."

"About locusts?"

"About a town that's plagued by locusts."

"I see."

They watched Tatyana. She tore at the reindeer's liver at the mouth of her ditch.

Nikitin opened his novel and said, "Dogs are the perfect animal."

Remedy

Milena Dumodova moved each one into the cold on her own. The cots screeched and left black stains across the floor. A few of the sick grabbed her by the shirtsleeve, pleading, and she took their wrists in a vice and told them next time she'd snap it in two. Some tried to knock over their IV bags, some rolled their eyes into their skull. Some acted like men.

They were all starving, so they weren't heavy. Twenty percent had grave injuries, meaning missing limbs, meaning no sweat. The rest had consumption or minor self-inflicted wounds. Slightly heavier. But she got all of them out into the little courtyard behind the hospital and lined them in neat rows and started her stopwatch.

The afternoon sky was low and gray. She unfolded a metal chair and sat and leaned her rifle against her thigh. The prisoners huddled under their blankets. They shook. They chattered. They made noise.

She cleared her throat and reached into her breast pocket and began pulling a frayed string from inside. She tugged at it, hand over hand, until the string snaked into a pile on the ground, and the thread was getting thicker, and she kept pulling, and the thread was almost as wide as the mouth of her pocket. A bulge formed in her pocket, and she gripped her coat with her left hand and pulled, red faced, with her right and the top of a human forehead materialized from the lip of the pocket, and it was a woman's face, and the woman's eyes were black, she was grimacing, and she bit the lip of the pocket, feisty, and

46

growled and Milena had to pry her teeth off with a pocket knife. The head spun and grumbled like a mouse caught by the tail. Milena flipped the pocket knife, catching it by the blade, and thumped the head between the eyes. It went dumb for a second, its tongue rolled out, then it blinked and smiled. Milena set the head on her shoulder and the two of them watched the freezing prisoners for the better part of an hour.

Milena jumped out of her chair when the door to the hospital opened. She turned and shrugged her shoulder and the head tumbled back into her breast pocket. Karriker stood with his hand still on the doorknob, looking at the rows of prisoners.

"What's this?"

Milena's hair was tied back in a severe bun. The wind had chapped her lips. "Moscow. Recent science. Fresh air cures all, they say."

"So."

"They have to be out here for an hour a day."

Karriker closed the door behind him. He walked along the rows of cots. "Some of these men are invalids."

"Well it wouldn't be fair to pick and choose."

Toward the back of the courtyard, a zek threw off his blankets and jumped and got his leg over the fence. Milena spun her rifle and fired and the man's thigh exploded and he tumbled to the other side of the fence. The rifle's barrel steamed. She shouldered it and said, "Do me a favor and push these boys in while I retrieve that patient."

Karriker pulled the first cot in. The prisoner's face was swollen black and blue. The second, the prisoner was alive, frantically rubbing his hands together.

Half of them were dead by the time he dragged them

47

into the relative warmth of the hospital.

Milena drank from the bottle and poured Karriker a glass. "Did you need more pills?"

The pridurok shook his head. "Just came to see you."

Milena took another drink, then stared at the bottle. Got up, got a smudged glass for herself, poured it. "You hate me."

Karriker's glass was untouched. "I don't."

"It's been…" she wiped a layer of dust from the ledger at her desk and thumbed through the pages. Closed it, tossed it in its place. "You don't come to see me. What am I supposed to think?"

The ocean sound of voices echoing in a hall. The scuffing of boots. Outside her office, four priduroks hauled frozen bodies to the mass grave. Karriker closed the door.

Milena's eyes narrowed. "You think that I have a choice?"

Karriker shrugged and drank his vodka.

Outside somebody cursed and laughed. Karriker reached across the desk and knocked over a picture of a Malamute. Milena watched him put it back in its place and poured the rest of her vodka into a glass. "Don't try to tell me that you don't have more."

"I do." The vodka dribbled down his chin. He swished the burn in his cheeks and smiled like a wolf.

Milena stared back at him. She heated up her oven. Lit some candles. "It's too cold."

Karriker hopped from his chair and slipped his fingers under her coat. "Hasn't stopped you, before."

She jumped like he electrocuted her. "Your fingers." She wrenched his hand away from her. She opened the door. Waved at it. "Don't come back without something to drink."

Karriker left. Milena closed the door and lit a cigarette and shook her hair out. She took her parka off and draped it over her chair. A spread eagle woman masturbated herself with a dildo on her left arm. The tattoo was framed by stars and guns and chicken feet. She made her rounds, checking vitals and handing out pills in sheer paper cups. On the clipboards tucked into the empty cots, she wrote "Did not respond to treatment." The zeks trembled as she passed. She retired to her quarters and blew smoke rings at the ceiling and that night she slept alone.

Competition

Hipolit won the ear pull the first night and kept his life, though once is never enough and soon he wreaked havoc, leaving a trail of severed ears in his wake. Three wins in as many days. The crowd fingered the crucifixes on their necks. They paced and they handed over cigarettes and threw caps to the floor. His most recent competition affected the posture of a radio operator, one hand clasped to the side of his face, the blood oozing through the cracks in the heel of his palm and dotting the floor. Wu tended to him quickly. He swabbed iodine and handed the zek a towel, and before the white cloth had been consumed by red he fell to his knees and picked the dripping ear off the floor. He made a five centimeter cut in the zek's side and swabbed it with iodine and stuffed the ear into the cut. He rolled a tube of gauze around the man's middle, then around his head. He set about fixing a bowl of opium.

Hipolit fell back against his cot. The shoe string was embedded in the thin skin between his ear and his skull. The blood coagulated. The shoestring melded with it. He made like he might pull it out but the pain was like a fire.

They slapped him on the leg. They knelt before him and offered him vodka and he picked his head off the pillow and drank for a long time. They set up a table in the corner for a card game and Hipolit turned over to go to sleep. His eyelashes didn't touch before they had him back on his feet and two zeks were restraining him. The shoelace dangled over his shoulder. The noise was overwhelming and he felt his guts churn and the dim lights were suddenly pulsing flames touching and he focused long enough to see a zek smiling big and his teeth were filed to points and in his hands he had a hand that didn't belong to him, and on the fingers there were metal tubes that he could hear shining in his ears and screwed into the end of each was a needle and the fingers were moving of their own accord, and the sharp-tooth prisoner held the wriggling appendage to Hipolit's chest and then the art began.

The Train

His throat sucked itself back into the open wound and Alek Karriker woke up to find one of his undershirts in tatters on the floor. He dressed and started a fire and smoked a cigarette and paced the room, waiting for the reveille. He picked up the ruined shirt and turned it over. Tatyana must have gotten in, somehow. But the cuts were too clean and he knew that it wasn't a dog.

He was about to leave when he saw what had happened to his shirt. The placenta lay flat on the desk, and the cloth had been cut and stitched to form a small diaper that covered nearly the entire slab of afterbirth.

Karriker didn't touch it.

He herded the zeks aimlessly. The world never found its balance. Something itched in his brain, in his throat, in his fingers. He talked to Nikitin and didn't say a thing about the clothed placenta and Nikitin talked about dogs and they watched Tatyana dig. He walked the old man back to his room like he did every day, and then set out for the train station, because today he had something to do.

The platform was empty except for four men nursing brass instruments. They never seemed to leave. They practiced and tuned and slept. All horn, all the time. Stravinsky in the key of rust. Karriker rubbed his hands together and nodded at them. An old man propped his tuba on the ground against his leg and waved a hand shiny with slide grease. A younger musician used a knife handle to crack the ice crusted on the valves of his French horn.

The train's headlights were a few minutes off. Karriker unlocked the door to the supply shed and batted at the dust motes that floated up to greet him. He pulled a thick ledger off of a shelf and tucked it under his arm and tilted a wooden desk sideways out of the shed and set it front and center of the platform. He set the ledger on the desk and went back to the supply shed to get a chair. He sat down. The train whistle got louder.

A uniformed gorilla with a moustache and an entourage of soldiers dragged tired boots and knuckles up to the platform, rubbing sleep from their eyes and sliding their tongues over unwashed teeth. One of the entourage had his cap tilted back and Karriker saw a tattoo—a skull with the tip of a pistol pointing from between its teeth—right between the soldier's eyes. The tattooed soldier mingled with his comrades. The gorilla gesticulated and joked. The tattooed man said nothing, but he stood in a semicircle with them while they laughed.

The train pulled in to the station, a bright red grill on a stunted, bi-lighted face. The lorries rocked side to side on their slats. Hands and feet hung from chicken wire windows. Shapes and faces.

The guards held their rifles in their hands and reached high into the sky, twisting and popping their lower backs. They ground cigarettes under their boots and cleared their throats.

Collective deep breath from the band for Tchaikovsky's "Waltz from Swan Lake."

The conductor shimmied the bolt off the lock. It clattered hollow on the wooden platform. The guards spat and their grips tightened and Karriker dabbed the pen in the inkwell to the right of the contracts.

The door rolled open and prisoners cascaded out. They shook out limbs. They pushed for air. They poked their ears against the brass din. They murmured amongst themselves.

The large soldier barked the loudest. He pushed at the throngs of prisoners, yelling at them to fall in. They lined up at Karriker's desk. The soldier shoved them if they strayed. Karriker handed pens to them and pushed papers across the desk to their waists, pointing at the different boxes and lines upon which they checked or signed. The prisoners moved around the side of the desk, but before they could be assigned to a truck, the gorilla blocked their way.

Karriker turned in his chair, "Comrade…"

"Shut the fuck up."

Karriker sighed and opened his mouth.

"I mean it, not a word."

He told the prisoners to strip and they hesitated only for a second, just to catch their breath. The blue wind chapped their bare backs. They stepped out of their pants and stood naked in the cold. The soldier inspected every inch of them. He grabbed one zek by the wrist forcefully and looked closely at the markings.

"You, over there."

He pointed to the east end of the platform. The prisoners with bare skin went west.

Ilya Bogrov approached the soldier carefully. The gorilla moved with the brevity and authority of a country doctor. The prisoners closed their eyes and turned out their lips to expose their hidden tattoos. The soldier put his face dangerously close to the hairy fault lines of their ass cracks and he stretched out their penises with a gloved hand to get the full impression of the permanent markings thereupon. "Go join your sisters," he'd say, and the tattooed repeat offenders would slink to their group.

Bogrov cleared his throat. "Excuse me, comrade."

"What?"

"Sir, it's just that I was noting that this is not a standard procedure."

"Who the fuck are you?"

Bogrov knew that he wasn't supposed to answer because it wasn't really a question.

The gorilla pointed at the ledger on Karriker's desk. "Fill out those papers as you would."

"Comrade Tarasov, may I ask what it is that you're doing?"

Tarasov, the gorilla, cracked his thumbs with his fists and got in Bogrov's face. "You can ask."

Bogrov said nothing.

"Camp's got to run smooth."

"I agree, sir."

"This isn't helping."

"Sorry, sir."

Bogrov stepped back and ignored the snickering of Tasarov's sycophants. He continued with his work. The band took a short rest and Karriker was halfway through. He pointed quickly at the lines the prisoners were to sign.

Once the zeks were processed Tasarov stomped through the snow to the transport trucks and sent the tattooed prisoners one way and sent the clear-skinned lot the other.

Karriker swept the platform and joked with the band. Tasarov and his group shoved each other and laughed. Bogrov smoked. Karriker shoved the table back into the shed and locked the door. Tasarov and his men jogged and chortled back to camp. Karriker spun the keys once on his finger and dropped them in his pocket. He saw the man with the forehead tattoo, staring into space and smoking, and he lit a smoke of his own and sidled next to him.

"Apraxin wouldn't like it."

Bogrov waved his smoke out of his face. He tossed his cigarette into the snow and left the platform without saying a word.

Anton Nikitin unfolded a *Pravda* and chewed a strip of deer jerky and held another out to Karriker who took it and turned it over in his hands and looked at it. He stared at the hole in front of him, deep enough now that he couldn't see the dog inside of it, only the metronome of flung tundra. Every couple of minutes Tatyana would pause from her digging and poke her head up, snout covered in dirt and tongue lolling, to make sure they were still there, then she'd get back to snuffling and tossing black dirt clods into the gray morning.

Nikitin chewed. "You know, I'm getting worried. Maybe annoyed."

"Why is that?"

"You remember what I said about dog's brains, having none of the bad parts?"

"I do."

He pointed at the hole with a gnawed strip of jerky. "This is a bad part."

Karriker leaned back in his stool and pulled his collar tighter. He pointed at the book Nikitin was cradling in his lap. "What are you reading?"

Mine Work

Not a solitary beam of sunlight made it into the cave. The miners' pupils swelled against the putrid red lamplight and squinted against the chunks and bits of dust they picked into their faces. The ground was flat and worn. Hipolit put his pick down and caressed the crusted shoestring in his ear. He picked the axe back up and went at the rock hard and didn't stop for an hour, hauling it in his arms to the mine cart and back again. Same as the day before, he didn't see a glint of gold. To his knowledge, no one ever had.

He scratched the gauze wrapped around his chest. During the day he felt thin rivulets of blood pool in his belly button and he hacked dust and wiped at the blood with the inside of his shirt.

When the gong struck and ricocheted down into the cave, Hipolit shouldered his axe and joined the rest of the blackened wraiths on their journey out. They stood in line and each of them sat in the bucket and listened to the groan of the rope and the creak of the pulley and prayed that it wouldn't snap and send them plummeting to their deaths.

Hipolit swung a leg out of the bucket and closed his eyes against the relative bright of the day. Pressed his hands hard into his eyes. Blinked. He stumbled past a crowd of smoking urki and climbed into the transport truck. His chest burned and his ears rang.

Wind knifed at the burlap cover. Ice swarmed and the prisoners huddled and no one talked.

Naked

Milena and Karriker sat naked on her cot. He was sweating and she was staring at the ceiling. He got up and lit a cigarette. The air was buzzing. Milena looked at his backside and reached over and slapped his ass. He almost dropped his cigarette.

"Too cold?"

Milena smiled.

He bit the cigarette and used both hands to roll her over and return the slap. She screamed and Karriker felt those close cousins, happiness, and the guilt of having such emotions in such a place.

Traced his finger along the curve of her back, along the tattoo etched on her spine. A goat-demon fucking a woman in the ass. He tapped his finger on it. "This," he said, "is a little distracting."

She twisted around, trying to see, and looked him dead in the eye. "You don't like it, baby? I can cut it off."

Her words dripped into his ears like liquid nitrogen. He said, "What is it for?"

"I broke a bitch's nose and the bitch had friends."

He spread her legs and kissed her thigh. He watched the beads of sweat roll and he looked at the tattoo above her shock of pubic hair, a few simple words: "Only 12 cm. cocks and up, please."

She caught him staring and caressed his cheek. "Oh, dear," she said, "Don't worry. I'll make an exception for you."

Chifir

The zeks measured the chifir with a matchbook and dumped the chopped leaves into their cups. They boiled a pot of water in the furnace. They listened to the pop of the water and the patter of snow outside. Tely Solokov bared his sharpened teeth and wrapped his hand in his shirt and pulled out the pot. He poured each of their cups and they stirred with their fingers and blew off the steam.

Hipolit was served last. He was stripped to the waist and the gauze was brown with blood. He put the smoky cup to his lips and he could see the explosion in his tonsils, could feel the tea force its way down his throat, cannonballing into the acids and bread crumbs in his stomach. His eyes shot up like blinds and the fault lines showed and he had to make a noise, this horrible whooping thing and all the other prisoners were making it too.

The noise congealed and became a cloud over them, and it pushed them out into the cold and the men lined up in front of a giant shelf of snow and they counted down and dove in tunneling to the other end of the shelf popping their heads out like moles and gnashing their teeth at the dragon scales in the sky and Hipolit chose not to tunnel he climbed on top of the barracks and tried to jump to the neighboring room but missed and hit his chin and bit his tongue and he was laughing and the blood was flowing and a few of the tunnelers stopped moving just horrible twisted heads in the snow and Hipolit thought I need to get out of here and they went inside and played cards and soon everyone was in their bunks not sleeping but masturbating furiously and Hipolit joined them and it was like a symphony of cicadas the dry chafing shaking and he didn't come but he didn't sleep either.

Ilya Bogrov Goes to Sleep

He melted snow and dipped his brush into the water and then into the baking soda. He brushed his teeth. He took off his uniform and hung it neatly in the closet and used the water to shave in the cracked mirror hanging on his wall. He studied his reflection. He sat at his bedside table and stared at the wall. He fell asleep on his right side, with his pillow folded over just so.

Chewed

Ilya Bogrov stood at attention. Karriker shut the door after him quietly. Bogrov stared at him and Karriker stepped to the other side of the cabin and didn't breathe. Apraxin sat in an Empire ormolu-mounted mahogany bergere behind his desk and ignored the both of them.

Karriker rocked back and forth on his heels. Bogrov was marble.

Finally, Apraxin said, without looking up, "Do you know why you're here?

"No, sir."

"Please explain, Comrade Karriker."

Karriker kept his eyes fixed on the ground. "Comrade Bogrov, three days ago you allowed Comrade Tasarov to move forward with an unregulated shift in transport and barracking."

Bogrov kept his mouth shut.

Apraxin smiled. "Under section H-234 of the criminal code you are guilty of aiding and abetting a traitor. You are hereby stripped of your position. You are to report to Comrade Karriker."

Bogrov did not bat an eye. "Yes, sir."

Apraxin picked lint off the razor edge of his cuff. He coughed into a silk handkerchief and waved at the floating spittle. "I have work for the two of you."

Bogrov kept his mouth shut. The silence hung for a second until Karriker caught his stare and caught on and cleared his throat and said, "Absolutely, sir."

"We have a rather strange problem on the East Urik

roadway." Apraxin rummaged through his papers and discovered what he needed and handed it across the desk to Karriker. "It's an all-day project. Don't worry about your prior obligations, you're covered."

Karriker's fingers had no sooner folded around the contours of the page when the door to Apraxin's office flung wide. Two malamutes the size of small moose traipsed in, a canvas tarp stretched between the two like a bridge, inside of which lay a tiny papoose inside of which was a brown face, just the eyes and the nose exposed around the cinched bindings.

The captain stood up so fast his chair tipped back behind him. A single oily lock of hair fell over his sweaty face. He rolled open a drawer and thrust the paper at the shaman and shouted, "If this is what you want, then by all means, *take it*." The Malamutes padded up to Apraxin, one gently taking the note from his fist, turned, and left.

After they were gone the three men were quiet for a long time. Bogrov stifled a sneeze and tried to will the dog hair off of him.

The tiny captain slid his glasses off his nose and pinched his eyes shut. The sun, which had been hidden behind slate gray clouds most of the day, came out. He put his glasses on and regarded the priduroks standing at attention at his desk.

"You both, I believe, have a job."

The Whale

Karriker shut the door and shielded his face against the cold. Bogrov stared at the snow and his nostrils flared and he reached up to his shoulder and tore the tassel from his uniform. He stripped himself of the patches signifying his rank. He took his cap and hurled it by its shiny brim into the snow. He kept his gloves and valenkis. Karriker buttoned his ushanka against the piercing wind and said, "That was stupid." Bogrov ran his hand over his thin hair and gave himself a couple slaps like he was batting at a fly.

The two of them crested a hill and started down the snowed-over path to the armory. They passed through the smoke from the kitchen and let the yeast stench soak into their clothes. The sky was the color of primer and the wind was making Bogrov's ears bright pink.

Two piles of snow like Roman rubble flanked the squat hut of the armory. There was a hut the size of an outhouse in front of it, and Karriker threw the door open without ceremony, startling the sleeping guard inside.

He wiped his eyes with his wrist. "What?"

"Dynamite."

"Who said?"

Karriker handed him the paper. He yawned and stepped out of the shadow of the hut to read it. Frowned, turned it over, handed it back. "This way."

Karriker turned back to Bogrov. "Cover your ears or you'll lose them."

Bogrov complied. He flipped his collar up and pressed the meat of his palms into his ears—now the color of hot pokers—like a petulant child.

The guard shivered and unlocked the padlock from the armory and the giant chain snaked to the ground and he kicked it out of the way so they could open the door.

The armory was a tiny building filled mostly with straw. A pile of rifles sat like kindling on a shelf. Boxes of grenades along the bottom. The guard rummaged a bit in the straw, eventually coming back with a burlap sack, sagging and bulging, and handed it over to them and was back in his hut and asleep before Karriker could finish counting the sticks of dynamite inside.

Bogrov stopped by his room for an ushanka. When he came back out he held a ring of tiny keys out to Karriker.

"What're those for?"

Bogrov tossed them. "The truck."

Karriker tossed them back. "I can't drive."

Bogrov jangled them against his thigh and looked at the sky and hopped into the driver's seat.

The tundra rolled outside his window. Karriker fingered the door handle. He wiped at the condensation inside the window.

"You know, comrade," he said, "I told Apraxin to go easy on you."

Bogrov's gloves creaked on the steering wheel. "You did?"

"I know why you didn't rat out Tasarov. I'm with you. Man was doing the right thing."

Bogrov looked in the rear view mirror. Snow spray.

"Those zeks, getting the same cages as the vors. It's just not fair. They eat them alive. Fuck that they're people. Even from an economic standpoint, Apraxin should thank

Tasarov. A worker who's not in constant fear of being raped or murdered will dig better, in the end."

Both men ignored the intense smell of fish that soon permeated the truck and wriggled between the threads in their clothes.

"I saw that wicked tattoo. On your forehead. Life's got its ups and downs doesn't it? Some days you wear your snappy uniform to work, other days you throw an axe."

The smell was everywhere now like a beach where everything was dead. Karriker coughed and turned red.

Bogrov drove on.

Bogrov shifted into park and the two of them sat for a while, letting the engine idle and the image in front of them sink in.

Karriker's mouth hung open. "What is that thing doing this far inland?"

Bogrov didn't answer.

They got out and let the tailgate down. Karriker jumped inside and grabbed the bag. They set it on the ground and Bogrov opened it and they sifted through the straw. Blasting caps, firing pins, wire, sticks.

Karriker grabbed some dynamite and started up the road. "Stinks."

Bogrov sniffed. "Yeah."

White afternoon light broke over the top of the thing's head, blinding. They moved closer into the mist and blinked away spots.

It was at least two tons. Pure snow all around it, none of it *on* it.

Karriker said, "I need another cigarette."

Its mouth was open, two rows of teeth like brushes

rustled in the breeze. Tongue heavy in the crepuscular maw. Marine stench came off the carcass in waves, its right half bone and green disease, its left half nearly intact. Beady eyes a solid vacant black.

Bogrov cupped his palms to light his cigarette. "Big fucking whale."

"Blue whale."

Ilya Bogrov smoked.

"Blue whales shouldn't even be close this time of year." Karriker moved closer to the thing to get shelter from the wind. A few meters from it, the wind died completely. He patted his pockets. Struck a match and the sound echoed and he stumbled back into the wind.

"It's winter. Blue whales have already migrated."

"Maybe this one was a straggler?"

"Whales migrate in a certain order. Old and pregnant whales first. Then the females, then the bulls, and finally the sexually immature males."

"And how would we find this out?"

"You curious?"

"I'm just here to blow it up."

"If you were interested, you'd need to do a gonadal investigation."

"Fuck that."

"Or an ear inspection. The ear plugs of mature and immature males are different."

Karriker walked around to the damaged right side. Viscera clung to most of the exposed ribs, the internal organs limp and moist under folds of blubber. A gash where the right flipper used to be. Karriker stuffed in a stick of dynamite. "Couldn't be the Inuits. They hunt whales, yes, but they use them."

"Ngansan?"

"No."

And like that the conversation died. Karriker bundled an armful of explosives and laid them in a row along the width of the whale's mouth. He placed some under the whale's weight along its flanks, making a nest of straw under each stick to keep the snow out. Bogrov stuck a fuse in each one and ran them all together and spooled the wire to a detonator. Karriker flipped up the safety and twisted the plunger and reached into his pocket and lit another smoke and sat on a half snowed over log.

Bogrov sat next to him. He wiped rotten blubber oil on the bark.

Karriker handed him a smoke and Bogrov took it. They watched their work, the whale wired up like it was under scientific study.

"Weirdest shit I've ever seen."

Bogrov thumbed the base of his cigarette and watched the ash float away.

"Wait, no, second weirdest shit I've ever seen."

Bogrov looked at him. "What was the first?"

"Apraxin, yelling at a couple of dogs and a midget Inuit."

After a time it seemed like Bogrov had let the conversation die again, but then, in a puff of smoke, he said, "That *was* weird."

Karriker turned to him. "Any idea what it was about?"

Bogrov scrunched up his face and shook his head, studying the cigarette as he ground it into the snow. "No."

And then, after a long time, Karriker said, "Are you going to kill me?"

Bogrov refrained from answering for a moment. "You're my superior."

"I wasn't the one who told Apraxin about Tasarov."

Bogrov turned to look at him with empty gray eyes. He cleared his throat and then the conversation really was dead. Karriker got up, wiping the snow off of his ass, and squatted in front of the plunger. He heard Bogrov walk up behind him. His nose having acclimated to the fish stink, all he could smell then was the crisp leather of those valenkis.

He heard Bogrov say, "Would you mind if I pushed it?"

Karriker stood up and gestured with his arm. "It's all yours, sir."

And Bogrov got on his haunches and wrapped his gloves around the plunger and took one last look at the blue whale smiling into nothingness.

Emergency Surgery

The hospital was empty. Imprints where the cots' legs had been. The windows were open, a white curtain fluttered in the dull wind. Dust motes floated in the sunlight. Karriker heard voices. He dropped the nearly lifeless body of Ilya Bogrov and ran to the back, threw open the door, went into the doctor's office. Empty. Desk was cluttered with paperwork. He went out the back and found Milena.

The beds were lined along the fence. Prisoners gripped blankets close to their chins. Teeth chattered. Beds rattled. Breath smoked.

Milena Dumodova rotated her gun barrel towards the sky and tucked the clipboard under her arm. "What's wrong?"

Karriker thumbed toward the door. "We had a little accident."

Placing her hand around the whale bone lodged firmly in Bogrov's upper thigh, Milena made eye contact with Karriker and counted down from five and on zero the tendons in her forearms popped and her hand slipped off the porcelain bone. Bogrov floated to the surface of consciousness long enough to emit a bloodcurdling howl and his ushanka fell off and it was like the tattoo was screaming. He weaved his head around and mumbled like a sleepwalker and passed out.

"Okay, let's try this again, shall we? This time, you grab the base."

He clutched the bone in both fists without so much as

a questioning glance. Milena rolled her lithe fingers around the top and counted down, and on zero they both pulled hard as they could and the bone made an awful sucking gravel sound and brought forth a geyser of blood that stained the white perfection of her smock, and Bogrov once again regained a split second of awareness to curse God.

Karriker watched her expertly apply a tourniquet and staunch the bleeding and dab the hole with bubbling brown disinfectant.

After Ilya Bogrov was safe and deep in sleep, Milena turned to Karriker and laced her fingers together. "Alek, did you dump a small mountain of opium in this man's wound?"

"Around it, yes. Where I could."

"Why?"

He ran his head over the stubble on his head and glanced at the comatose pridurok, pointing at the small smile on his lips. "He doesn't seem to mind."

"Is he an addict?"

"Nah. Clean as the snow. Kind of a buzz kill, this one."

"Fuck, Alek. He could OD."

"I don't think *anyone* in camp has ever even owned enough opium to overdose. Calm down." He reached to stroke the side of her face and she pulled away but didn't seem overly annoyed. "I wonder how many escaped."

They put on their overcoats and threw the backdoor wide and began moving amongst the blue zeks. Some of them were only a pair of eyes peeking out from the cave of their blue wool prison blankets, others' heads poked from their cocoons, chattering teeth and blinking erratically. Three beds were empty and Milena cursed under her breath and made markings on her clipboard. Karriker stuffed his hands in his pockets and looked to the sky.

A few beds down, a zek removed his blanket to reveal a foot missing three toes. It was turning black. He called out that he needed to go back inside. Milena didn't flinch. She punched a hand in the air, extravagantly moving the heavy black cuffs of her overcoat out of the way of her watch. "Five minutes."

She turned to Karriker and said, "You stink," and Karriker smiled with a cigarette in his lips and turned from the wind to cup a match. She looked at her watch again and shouted at the zeks that they were free to move back inside, and they exploded, the blankets flying off, the prisoners moving as quickly as their frozen bones would let them, to get some heat going. They got into fistfights over who got to push his bed in first. Karriker said, "They're more active than last time."

Milena watched the show. "Treatment's working."

Karriker was sitting at her desk and she offered him a drink and slipped out of her tunic and Karriker saw the tattoos riddled over her right forearm. He grabbed her and pulled her down on top of him. Toed the door shut.

She smiled. Her teeth were sharp. She kissed him. "Where have you been?"

"Busy."

"Don't lie to me."

"Most times I'm free you're here. Busy." Holding up his arm. "Busy."

"Blowing things up?"

"Blowing things up, yes. Generally restoring order. Being official."

"Weak."

"How many men are you planning on freezing to death?"

Her fingers brushed the ridges of his scar, his chin, his lips. "Are you coming to see me tonight?"

"When?"

Milena nodded at the closed door. "When the kids are asleep."

Karriker eyed her cot against the opposite wall. "I'll be here."

Heartless

Hipolit opened his eyes and sat straight up in bed. He grasped at his chest and it felt empty. He saw the form of it under his blankets, and he threw them back and recoiled and recovered and began to pick blue lint out of the ventricles of his heart. He blew on it and it pumped happily at his touch. He dropped it into the black hole in his chest and the skin closed around it like quicksand swallowing someone to the fingertips and then he stood up and paced the empty floorboards of his barracks.

He wasn't alone. Tely sat in the corner, in the shadows, and smoked and watched Hipolit, the shoestring still stuck in the back of his ear, grafted, a strange charm. He placed the cigarette carefully between his filed teeth and crossed his legs. "Our champion is awake."

Hipolit jumped and spun. He held his hand over his chest and smiled sheepishly. "It doesn't hurt so bad, now."

"That's good." Like he had already forgotten. "There is a pressing issue at hand, though."

Hipolit felt at the shoestring and touched his ear gingerly. "What?"

Tely got up and moved to him, the sound like sand rushing from a broken hourglass. "The bitch. The suka."

Hipolit put the shoestring in his mouth and sucked on it. "I don't know him, I already told you."

Tely knelt in front of him. "He wears things that he should not. He has been marked, and he deserved them, once. But not anymore. He is not who his tattoos claim.

That has to be fixed. The organization has told me that they are done dealing with sukas. The *vory v zakone* must be respected, we must uphold some standard of loyalty, we must punish those who can't uphold a simple code. We will kill them as they come. The train comes in and if they have picked up a rifle, we will kill them. If they've sworn their allegiances elsewhere, we will kill them."

Hipolit chewed. "So, you're going to kill the suka."

Tely showed his sharp teeth. "This is war. We're going to kill him twice."

Hipolit nodded and spit out the shoestring.

Friends

When he got to the hospital Bogrov was sleeping. His dressings were fresh. Karriker changed the bottle from one hand to another and looked at him for a moment, then walked away. The patients were silent. Some stared at lamplight flickering across the ceiling, others feigned at sleep and still others were deeply sedated.

He found Milena towards the back, near her office. She covered a body with a white sheet and started when he said her name. Sweat poured from her temples. The way her shirtsleeves were rolled up, it almost seemed as though she had been tilling a garden. Small scratches irritated her skin, but there was no blood. She walked quickly to her office and Karriker took one last look at the white sheet and headed after her.

The bottle had no sooner touched her desk then she scooped it up and popped the cork and drank. The liquor made her redder.

Karriker took a seat and crossed his legs. "And how was your day?"

Milena stared at him for a moment. She moved around to the other side of her desk and sat down. She unrolled her desk drawer and set out two cups, then two more. Poured each to the brim. She swirled the vodka in its bottle and frowned. Got up and opened a cabinet. Set two bowls on the table and filled them each almost to brimming with the vodka, then downed the last gulp. Then, without a pause, she flipped the bottle over and caught it by the handle and threw it with force at Karriker's head.

It bounced off his temple and he said, "Fuck!" and fell off his chair. The thick glass clattered on the floor but did not break. Milena scooped it up and hit him twice in the back until the only thing visible over the desk was Karriker's empty hands, pleading with her to stop, wavering back and forth, trying to determine from which direction the next blow might come. Milena faked to the left, then to the right, the frantic hands following her trajectory and clasping at air. Karriker whimpered.

Abruptly she turned her back and flung the door open and let the bottle sail into the dark infirmary, and when she closed the door in the silence they heard the bottle break, muffled to the sound of pocket change jingling, and she went around the desk, unable to resist first making like she'd kick him again, then sat down and brought one of the fuming bowls to her lips, the vodka pouring from both sides of her mouth like a clumsy child finishing the milk in a cereal bowl.

Karriker crawled from the floor, eyes wide, palm pressed firmly on his wounded temple, onto his chair. Leaned back and focused on breathing. Milena set the bowl down, empty, and wiped her lips, and stared at him for a moment, and finally nudged one of the glasses at him.

He brought it with his trembling palms to his lips and it cleared his head and the two of them smiled at each other like devils from across the table.

Card Game

Hipolit lost everything quickly. He sat at the edge of the crowd, feeling the heat of the bodies around him, watching Tely and four men glare at each other over their cards, watched the inquisitive way they turned their heads to smoke their cigarettes, the squint of their eyes down to slits when the moment was tense. All four of them wore crucifixes around their necks. They were all shirtless, baring their stories to each other, struggling to appear open as they laughed and lied.

He sucked the string in his ear. No one had challenged him in a week's time, and as such they'd moved on to other pursuits. Cards, anyone could win. Skill was crippled by luck and that made each game entertaining. Hipolit was Heartless and they let him play the game but his talent for cards stood at the opposite end of the spectrum from that of his ear pull. He had won a surplus of cigarettes that he didn't smoke and gave them up in the card game without protest, only sweating when it seemed that he would run out and not be able to participate any longer.

Tely was the next one to lose, he'd put all of his cigarettes in on a bluff and a Ukranian named Rudy raked them in with a cackling laugh and Tely sat back in his chair and turned a bright red and caught the wrist of the man to his left, stopping him from dealing the next hand.

"My cards. If I'm not in the game, then." He made to grab them and the dealer elbowed him out of the way. The crowd booed. Tely sat back and threw his hands up and licked his teeth. His eyes narrowed at Rudy.

"Good hand."

Rudy didn't answer. Nodded then turned his attention back to the cards.

Hipolit watched Tely lean back, watched him smile with his shark teeth. The chair groaned under the strain. Tely leaned forward and the chair's legs cracked onto the floor. "Let me buy back in."

The dealer sighed and scratched a sore in the hollow of his clavicle. "No buy backs, Tely."

Tely opened his palm. "Come on, they are my cards and I organized this game, I should be—"

Rudy beat his fist on the table. Cigarettes rolled off and vors leaned down swiftly to scoop them.

Tely rested his elbow on the table. Lifted his hand up and rubbed his fingers together. The room was quiet. Rudy continued. "Let us finish this game in peace."

Tely stood up and pushed his chair in. He walked into the crowd and stood next to Hipolit and the two of them watched the next few hands in silence. Rudy's luck ran out soon thereafter, and he tossed in the last of his cigarettes and kissed them goodbye. As he stood up from the table, Tely made his move. He sidled next to the Ukrainian and slapped him on the back. "I apologize for my behavior, it was out of line."

Rudy said nothing. He pushed Tely's hand off of his back. "Don't touch me."

Tely said, loud enough for the crowd to hear. "Tough luck with those cards, my friend."

The Uke kept quiet. He threw on his jacket and motioned to his crew and the five of them walked out into the night. Tely followed. Hipolit said a prayer and followed.

The first mistake his friend made was the force with

which he opened the door. It nearly came off its hinges and he bounded down the steps like a bull. The group of Ukrainians had more than enough time to prepare. The second mistake Tely made was in the way he hit, his fist lumbering out of the air, on a wobbly trajectory for Rudy's mouth. Rudy ducked it and brought his closed hand into Tely's stomach and the vor crumbled. The third mistake was bringing Hipolit. The Pole kept to the outside of the crowd. Two of the Uke's watched him and spat at his feet while Rudy and two others kicked the shit out of Tely.

The Ukrainians got cold and left the wheezing body in the snow. The two men watching Hipolit looked over their shoulders, noted their friends leaving, and gave one last look at Hipolit. One of them smacked him in the face. They laughed and headed after their pack.

Hipolit nursed his nose and pulled Tely out of the snow, his friend who had at first seemed so frightening, now beaten all to hell. He wrapped his friends arm over his neck and the wind chapped their faces and Tely broke away from him and headed back into the barracks.

The two remaining card players were the only zeks that didn't look at him. His right eye was a black mess, his nose and mouth dripped blood. A cut on his head. Most of the vors laughed.

Tely leaned against the wall until the game had finished, then he scooped his cards into a pile and pocketed them and the two of them went out and shared a cigarette in the snow.

"I've had a run of bad luck, lately." At least that's what Hipolit heard, through his friend's broken teeth. He nodded.

"I have no respect anymore, Hipolit. No one respects

me. Why else would they put me in charge of you?"

Hipolit smoked. "Sorry."

"Why *me*? After all I've done for them."

"Maybe your luck will change."

Tely tapped Hipolit's chest. "How is it healing?"

"Fine."

"I should have seen it."

"I'm sorry."

"Stop apologizing, idiot."

"Maybe your luck will change."

"We make our own luck, Polack." The match flared and he touched it to the cigarette. He nodded to the building in front of them.

They were standing in front of the schoolhouse, the word "suka" in big white painted letters on the side. Hipolit knew what was going to happen, and he had to focus on standing still, on ignoring the voice that called from deep inside himself, to run as fast as he could, without looking back.

Regret

&

Friends Share a Smoke

The next morning Alek Karriker sat smoking and talking literature with Nikitin. The old man had Tatyana by her leash and every muscle on the dog was tense. Nikitin had filled in the hole and the dog stared at the fresh-packed dirt like an addict.

Taking advantage of a lull in the conversation, Karriker said, "Milena nearly beat me to death last night."

"I saw the bruises, but I wasn't going to say anything."

"She's got a temper."

Nikitin scratched the scruff of Tatyana's neck.

"I don't know what to do."

"I don't know much about women," Nikitin tapped a gnarled paperback against his thigh.

"Me neither."

They stared at the covered pit. Karriker said, "Aren't you even a little curious?"

The old man dragged his thumb across the closed pages. "No."

Tatyana began to sniff the covered-up pit and she took a tentative swipe at the dirt and Nikitin launched out of his chair with energy Karriker had never seen and he kicked the dog in the ribs and she gave a little yip and a snarl and he sat back down and she went to him and nuzzled his palm and he gave her a pat on the belly and she laid down.

"First time I've seen you do that."

Nikitin didn't answer but when he turned in he let Tatyana climb onto the bed.

Karriker picked up opium from Wu and brought it to Bogrov. The two of them sat and smoked in relative silence. Bogrov occasionally bent his leg and massaged his thigh. The two of them laughed once or twice.

Death Squad
&
the Cut on
Karriker's Throat

Later that night Milena ran her hand over Karriker's chest and talked about her mother. "I had been closer to my father. My father was a good man. He worked for the Commisarat. Then my mother died in Stalingrad. They say many women on the Death Squad did not make it back. One time, I saw a picture of her in the paper with Shalya Shostakovich. It was a big deal to everyone but me. When we got the news of her death my father and I started wearing her clothes. It was strange, my father and I hated coffee but we each started drinking it in the morning. Father grew his hair long and kept it cinched in a bun. I did the same. I liked her better after that. Better than my father. Her ghost, at least."

Karriker smiled at her. "Where is your father now?"

Milena laid her head on his chest. "As far as I know, he's still in the old house. He doesn't like to go out. There's a corner store just down the street. Far as I know that's his only trip on any given day. He stays in there and listens to his neighbors and calls the police if he hears anything he feels might be dangerous."

"Does he miss you?"

"I get letters from him every month or so."

"Do you miss him?"

She was quiet for a long time. "I miss him very much."

She touched Karriker's scar. "How did you get this?"

Karriker thought about it for a moment. The air was velvet with the smell of flowers, a perfume that Milena had never put on before that night. He lit a cigarette and the smoke overwhelmed the perfume like squid ink in an ocean of pheromones.

"This? Fucker who did this was an amateur." He smoked for a while, as though that was enough of an explanation. He caught her eye and went on. "He came up from behind and tilted my head back like in the movies, dragging a razor between the jugular and carotid, emptying enough blood to be scary but not enough to kill me. I remember the snow on my cheek and the blood was brown. I stood up, I was very dizzy, and I took off my shirt and pressed it like this, the blood was warm and it soaked into the cloth. My hands were shaking. No one was there. I was at the Rosijja, it was a great place for tourists, and the bellhop knew me, he'd run me off before, and he saw the blood and his eyes went like this and he ran back into the hotel. On any other day the manager would have kicked my ass into the river himself, but that happened to be the day that Diego Rivera was there, in the hotel lobby. He was at the counter, flirting with the clerk. I was lucky. If the most famous socialist realist painter in the world saw him kicking a poor dying man into the freezing river, his job, gone. So he screamed till his face turned red, 'someone, get a fucking ambulance,' and the bellhop had said, 'citizen, do you know who this is?' And the manager said, 'yes,

I fucking well know who it is.' Diego asked *who* it was exactly, threatening, and the hotel manager turned purple and said, 'A man in need of an ambulance, where is that ambulance?'"

Milena smiled. "Do you remember what you did to deserve it?"

"No one deserves that. It was truly horrible."

"But what did you do?"

"I honestly do not remember."

Milena didn't push the issue. The two of them fell asleep together.

Another Dead Animal

On his walk back to his schoolhouse, sometime before the reveille, Karriker's path was blocked by another dead animal. He approached it slowly, sweat beading on his forehead, boots stomping in the melted snow, and soon he realized that the animal was in fact not a deer, but a dog, and that the dog had concentric circles shaved into its fur. He fell to his knees. He gripped his skull and wondered if his friend wasn't already out looking for it. He grabbed it in both arms and lugged it into his room. It made the room hot. He picked it back up and carried it the same way he carried dead prisoners, through the alley and up the hill, and he dumped it into the shallow grave and was halfway down the hill when an idea struck him. He almost pushed it out of his mind, almost retreated to his room without looking back, but the itch in his brain got the best of him and he climbed the hill and dug into the slit in Tatyana's middle and found nothing. Except for the placenta. He pulled it out and tucked it into his chest and ran back to his barracks, falling once in the snow.

That morning he did not sleep. He set the placenta on his desk, just as he had before, and he stared at it until he heard the reveille.

He found Nikitin by his stool without a book, staring into the distance.

Karriker didn't say anything. He sat by the old man and the two of them watched the sun come up.

87

Finally, Nikitin wet his lips and said, "I should not have kicked her like I did. Dog's brain's have a strong sense of loyalty, and that loyalty was betrayed when I did what I did. I do not deserve her company, and I hope that wherever she is, she's happy. Yesterday we caught a young man who was trying to escape. We should have turned him in and I knew that that was my job, but the dog looked at me and I could tell, I do not want to say it was telepathic, but I sensed very strongly that she did not want me to turn the zek in, that it would have killed him and she didn't want to see him dead. So I didn't, I let him go, and he thanked me over and over, he had the worst little Polish accent I'd ever heard, and I told him to sit down and so he did, and sure enough it seemed like Tatyana really liked him. And he said that he was no killer and that he couldn't live in a place this evil, that had this many killers. That he could feel himself, not becoming a killer but forced, like gravity he said, but his Russian was very bad, pulled into these actions and that he knew that if he didn't leave he would have to do something horrible, which he did not want to do. So I let him go and I felt that when he was gone Tatyana," he hadn't spoken her name up till then, and his voice cracked, "had forgiven me for my violence, and in a way I understood that this place makes you crazy, it's making that boy crazy and it made my dog crazy and I tried to fight it and now she's gone."

He smoked opium with Bogrov and he fell asleep sitting in the chair. Bogrov did not wake him up and finished the entire cigarette himself. When Karriker finally snapped awake Bogrov grinned and they both laughed. They continued like that for the next few days. Karriker would stay up all night, reading and making cards and smoking and keeping an eye on the placenta drying on his desk, then finally catch a nap in the afternoon, the gray sky brightening the curtains, the dust motes twirling around his face, and Bogrov would smoke the whole cigarette every time, and his leg was getting better and better but he was smoking the powder more and more. Karriker would wake up and stumble over to Milena's office and the two of them would talk until night fell and some nights, when he was exhausted, Karriker would stay there and stumble home before the wake-up call, and on the fifth day he went home too early and the placenta started to hum at his desk and he felt the heat on his throat.

He pinned his eyes open with his fingers but sleep draped over him like blindness. He woke up in his bed. He was dressed. Wiped the drool from his lip. He stood and let his eyes adjust and the entire room was covered in cryptic chalk language. He spit on the floor because it hurt too bad to swallow. Focused on breathing. The chalk writing on the walls was big and declarative, but it got smaller and more pointed as it got closer to his desk, as if that point in space was a drain, sucking all of the life and creative energy into it and returning nothing but questions.

Tatyana's placenta was decorated in colorful beads and cloth. Another piece of cloth was cut to ribbons on the floor, and he groaned and picked up what was left of the colorful bag the Ngansan had given him, in which he stored his opium, now in a pile dusting between the floorboards.

He tried his best to get through his day normally. He did his job, there was no train. He sat with Nikitin and neither of them said a word, which was fine by him. He sat and smoked with Bogrov, and his friend seemed concerned at his silence, maybe at something behind his eyes, and this was the first emotion from Bogrov outside of a smile that Karriker had ever seen. He spent time with Milena and she seemed distracted and he left early. Walked back to his room and covered against the wind. For a brief moment he wondered how much longer he could stand to be in the camp.

When he opened the door the placenta was gone. The chalk writing still screamed at him.

Attempted Escape
&
Mine Accident

Hipolit said nothing to anyone. The rattle of tools and the clink of pick on rock sounded like a busy kitchen.

He packed his knapsack with a couple loaves of black bread.

He waited until the day was over. Fire pumped in his muscles, vision charged with oppressive static that only seemed to disperse around soft things, places to rest the head.

He looked both ways before he left his bunk. He appropriated a wheelbarrow left resting beside a barrack. The guards looked at the wheelbarrow and looked away. He followed the barbed wire all the way around the camp. All the posts were buried a meter underground. The wire was thick, strung centimeters apart to that same meter's depth. He followed the track his wheelbarrow made around the perimeter twice. Leaned against a barrack and tried to catch his breath. Stars of barbed wire floated in his face like gnats. The wires tunneled like moles beneath the surface, following him wherever he walked. A guard asked him what he thought he was doing. He said he lost his wheelbarrow and the soldier told him if he saw him again without it he'd be sorry.

When he returned to it the handles were wrapped

91

tight with wire. The wheels were flat with metal stars. His way was blocked where it hadn't been minutes before. He couldn't go back to his room, the barracks were corseted in barbed wire. He heard the sound, a rope of wire as thick as a tree trunk broke the surface just beyond the perimeter and blocked out the sun and came down hard on the other side of camp. Tightened like a snake. The camp squeezed, the back of it becoming pinpoints, the front expanding and distorting. If he walked toward it he could feel himself shrink. So he went the other way.

He was caught just outside the sally port. The old man shook him out of his stupor and life returned to his face. The old man said nothing, simply pointed him back to camp, back to his bed, something soft. There was a dog there, a poorly groomed German Shepherd that had licked his hand.

Days went by and waves of relief and nausea fought over him.

He sat in circles with tattooed men. They played cards and growled at each other. He lost cigarettes. He misunderstood jokes. He started to smell like them. They shared their vodka with him and it left him balled up and puking. The big crucifixes they wore around their necks hit him in the face as they lifted him and rolled him onto his cot. When he woke in the morning with the reveille Tely smiled at him and asked him how he felt. Told him he wasn't working, just stand up and be counted. After he laid back down, Tely talked about the suka. About what they were going to do.

His anger at Alek Karriker became a red hot poker that had sizzled in the Siberian ice and steamed and blinded him and when the smoke cleared he looked down at his chest and felt his heart scuttling around his guts like a rat in a bag of deer meat and he wondered how he'd gotten there. The answer stood in front of him like something giant that he was already touching the corner of, that stretched out into the stars. It scared him. He needed to get out.

The next day he worked because he heard himself laugh and when he tongued his teeth the points drew blood. He worked hard in the lamplight of the cave. He threw his pick and scratched at the shoelace still lodged in his ear. Pulled at it. The string hurt like a fire. The skin that grew over it was fishbelly pale. He dug at it with his nail. Winced. A lantern swung from a pulley system built into the rock. Hipolit listened to the creak of it, gentle, and pictured himself on a boat somewhere, which lasted only for a second, as the heavy dust of the mine got in his lungs and he could no longer imagine the smell of salt. He beat the pick into the rock until sparks showed. Felt the frustration rising in his guts. He felt how sharp his teeth were. He pivoted his hips and swung the pick up into the lantern, plunging the mine into darkness so thick it brought everyone together, the sound of everyone's breathing and voices pushing against each other. He bent down. Felt the ground with his head in the air, eyes wide. Felt the smooth shard of glass. Scooped it from the dirt. Pressed it to the fishbelly skin over the lace and applied pressure.

Up the mineshaft, a zek frantically searched for the notch to tie off his mine cart. The rope slipped out and the pulley screamed and the metal box screeched down the tunnel. Hipolit's skin opened and he dug out the lace and he felt the breeze of the cart blowing past him and heard the meaty smack of it, drowning out the frightened screams, covering him in warm blood.

In Which Ilya Bogrov Feels Conflicted

The floor hummed. The heel of his foot touched volcanic. Pain gestated in waves before shooting into his brain. He'd swam out of the soup earlier, and everything had an edge now, everything was a cog in a system that ran too sharp, too smooth.

Opium. Bogrov walked his bed from head to foot. White knuckle on the metal frame. Hospital held its breath. There were no eyes on him. Everyone in the room was dead or catatonic or praying that Milena would stay in her office. He walked to the head of the bed.

Today you can walk.

Opium. He stretched and breathed and did a few push-ups. His leg wobbled like a rope bridge. He passed out onto his stomach and woke up with his cheek stuck to the floor. Rolled over, kneaded his fingers in his thigh. A door opened, the room gasped. Milena set down her clipboard and grabbed Bogrov under the arms and lifted him into bed. Gave him pills for his tuberculosis and he thanked her.

Opium. Karriker.

"Have you seen Alek today?"

"Do you need something for the pain?"

Ilya Bogrov placed his hands under his knee and lifted. "No. Just wondering if you'd seen him."

Milena kept her eyes on her chart. "If you need morphine, let me know. Or ask the Chinaman."

94

"Why is he here?"

"Who? Wu?"

"You dispense morphine. What purpose does he serve?"

"You talk weird."

"Why is he here?"

"Have you met my boss?"

"Yes."

"Yesterday he called me into his office to go over casualty reports. For the new treatment. He had a pair of dentures in his hand that he was using to nudge what I can only hope was an animal's heart. So there's the first answer. Secondly, Stalin's dead."

"I know."

"Stalin's dead and the camps, especially the gold mining camps, are turning into legitimate mining towns. You've heard of Snezhinsk? On the sea? Stalin's body isn't cold and that town is booming. Apraxin sees himself as the mayor of wherever here is. I'm the doctor. Wu is the medicine man. Why do you think they let Alek sell bread to the zeks who can't earn it?"

"He's the general store."

"He will be. This town was built as a model for when the Americans came. They could inspect the schoolhouse and see all the children learning and it looked like a town. Then when they left the wire could go back up and here we are."

"It would be hard to sell your wares with all that graffiti."

"I don't know why he never washes that stuff off. The vors want to kill him. He's a suka. A traitor. But they would have done the same if they'd had the opportunity."

"Not all of them would."

"Do you want morphine or not?"

Bogrov swallowed. Sweat beaded on his forehead. "Has Alek always used the powder?"

"I don't know."

"How often do you see him use it?"

"I don't know. I'm not his mother. Do you want the morphine or do you want to walk to the Chinaman's?"

"Neither."

"No?"

"No."

"Good idea. Best not to let yourself get addicted." She turned to walk away.

"If you see Alek, just tell him I'm here."

"Are you gay?"

"We're friends."

Milena stared. "I'll tell him."

Time got murky and Bogrov stared at the ceiling. He traced a line in the dust on his cot. Heard the snow creak outside. Counted breaths. Everything was black and quiet, and then, torpedoed from the depths of the void, a whale bone, smooth and gleaming, until his vision was clogged with staggering white light. Eyes snapped open: he wiped his forehead and sat up and flung his legs over the side of his mattress and felt the pain all the way in his molars. Told himself to love it. His bed shook where he supported himself. Thick blue veins in his forearm. Snatched his clothes from their pile under his cot and lifted his good leg in, shaking his bad leg in and biting his bottom lip, a thin rivulet of spittle flung to the floor.

His blanket was crumpled in a corner of the bed. He bent and pulled it smooth over the cot, felt the creases out. He stood back up and the pain flooded back in. He put on his coat and hat and dropped a couple cigarettes in his pocket and headed into the cold. Blue wind tore through the barracks, snow drifts up to the windows. Teeth chattered and he knotted his jaw.

He smoked a cigarette and limped around the camp. The pain had grown too big to notice. Acknowledging it meant collapse.

At the edge of camp he plucked a taut string on the barbed wire. A transparent ellipse vibrated down the line. He sat on a stoop between two drifts of snow and bounced his good leg. Smoked. Paced. He walked to Wu's barracks and stopped at the door. His body screamed. He could see Karriker putting the powder into the rolling papers. He took off his ushanka and sat on the stoop and watched a few privileged prisoners running errands around the camp, carrying notes or hammering plywood together or pretending to work. He saw Karriker lighting the cigarette. The smell. He rubbed the screaming skull on his forehead and the wind made his nose run. Wiped the snot and stared at it on his glove. Couldn't stop his teeth from clicking. He pounded his fist.

The pain in his leg was like a small, rabid animal trapped in a latex bubble, clawing around in it, the paws and claws stretching the material into thin pinpoints of agony and the cold did nothing for it. The sky was a bag of steel wool dumped over a half-frozen lake.

He felt the curve of his hip, feeling for his weapon like a phantom limb. He reached into his holster and felt the inner seams that bound the leather and his nerves calmed. He left Wu's front step and limped toward the hospital. He was halfway there when a sound caught his attention.

Like meat on a grill. Between a pair of barracks, a soldier with a slight hunch was urinating in the snow. The stream flowed strong. Bogrov's eyes floated up and locked on the young man's hips. Steam rose. The dirty black of the *Makarov* lashed against the young guard's leg. He ran his tongue over his teeth.

His valenkis crunched in the snow. The hurt leg was dead weight but he did his best to keep it quiet. Closer he got the stronger the smell of ammonia. Steadied his breath. He used both hands on his thigh to place his leg gently on the ground. Bogrov had never seen anyone take a piss like the guard. He reached out his right arm toward the boy. The soldier tilted his head back and moaned. Without his hand for support, Bogrov's leg fell heavy, and the pain took on a new flavor, and Bogrov grunted. The young guard cocked his head and, still pissing, turned, staining Ilya Bogrov's legs dark. The two of them stared at the scene for a moment, the piss flowing over the wounded leg, and the private laughed like a child. Bogrov jabbed his right hand out quickly. The soldier swatted it away like a fly. Bogrov stepped out with his right leg for balance and screamed and fell.

The guard wrapped his left arm around Bogrov as though they were old friends and tightened his grip. Bogrov gagged against his choke hold and the boy was still pissing, now all over Bogrov's ass. Bogrov fell to his knees and felt his eyes getting dimmer. His eyes bulged and he grabbed at the empty space. He reached back, trying to grab the boy's face and the guard lifted a mothering hand and pushed his claw away. He heard the soldier whispering something to him. The pissing stopped. Bogrov's eyes began to close.

His fingers dipping into the slush of snow roused him for a second. Oxygen was a distant memory. Face sweated purple. The kid was looking around for comrades, for friends to share the moment. Bogrov's fingers felt the snow, the cool crunching beneath his fingers. He closed a fist around the cold powder and slipped his hand as though to scratch the small of his back. The guard's penis hung from the cave of his pants, slightly aroused from rubbing against Bogrov's uniform. Bogrov gritted his teeth and wrapped his fistful of snow around the soldier's exposed cock. For a second nothing happened, then the guard tried to slap his hand away, and then he screamed and let him go.

While the boy stuffed his dick in his pants, Bogrov caught his breath. The soldier scrambled to his feet and reached his leg back for a kick. When he followed through Bogrov caught the limb under his arm and fell hard, putting all his weight on the guard's knee. The leg broke. The soldier screamed and waved his arms. Bogrov crawled onto him and punched him three times in the throat. He died quickly.

Bogrov rolled over and caught his breath. The temporary warmth of the urine froze and stuck to his skin. Slid the Makarov from the man's belt. The corpse was already turning blue. He stood on numb hunks of putty. Fell into the side of a barracks. The reek of ammonia. He gritted his teeth and pulled himself up.

Karriker and Nikitin sat in Nikitin's room, watching the oven.

Nikitin's face had fewer wrinkles. "I haven't read anything in a while."

Karriker smoked. "Me neither."

"Nothing seems interesting. Or it is interesting, but it is all like you said. None of it is real."

Karriker didn't say anything.

"Last night I heard from her."

"Who?"

"The voice was different. Normally when I hear the sound it's static. Radio noise. Coded. Last night it was something different. It was feelings. Never felt them before. Or I have, but different. Not as pure. Warm and red feelings. She was trying to tell me something."

Karriker burned his finger.

"She wanted me to know that she didn't leave because of what I had done. She loved me. Those were the colors. They were love. But this place was not for her. She was too good for it. There is too much love in her. There is a pack of wolves that hunts this area, hunts the reindeer. She is with them. Dogs are their instincts, I get that now. Because of the feelings."

A log cracked in the stove. Smell of sweat and dead skin. Karriker slouched in his chair. "At least she doesn't blame you."

They sat like that for a while and Anton Nikitin fell asleep in his chair.

Hipolit came out of the mines and looked at the landscape of blue ice. To the east there was a tangle of scrub and a bird sat motionless. Hipolit stared at it. The wind blew the scrub and the thing on the branch didn't move. Snow flurries blurred the horizon and when it cleared the bird was still there. He was in a soundless vacuum. There was only the gray sky and the scrub and this bird. It sat on the branch stock still, and then, with a sound like a whale cresting the surface, the bird flitted from one branch to another. The silence that surrounded him was like a glass bubble, and he could see the bubble rising to a point in the sky, then it left the earth, chunks of snow and ice falling off of its sheer edge, and it drained into a point in the sky and shot down into his skull like a blast of hot water and he could hear the guard shouting in his face and the zeks shouting and pointing dirty fingernails. Wiped the blood out of his eyes. The soldier had a high-pitched voice and a full beard and his Russian was so fast that Hipolit decided to ignore it completely.

The soldier turned bright red and caught Hipolit in the cheek with the butt of his rifle. Hipolit cupped his palm to his face. Fresh blood moisturized the dried dirt. Dripped between his fingers. The zeks watched, turtled in their bulky coats. Hipolit, standing there, existing, enraged the guard. He prepped for a second strike.

Hipolit wiped the blood on his pants and took off his shirt. The crowd stepped back.

The sound of the bandages tearing was impossibly loud. Frayed filthy ribbons coasted to the ground. His chest turned blue in the Siberian air.

The guard studied the art on Hipolit's chest. Knotted jaw. Protein deficiency the only savior of his rifle's integrity.

Hipolit redressed.

They loaded into the trucks. No one talked. The engines gunned. The bird was gone.

The zeks exited the trucks and waited in line for their slip. Proof that they'd done enough work to earn a bread ration. Hipolit shuffled to the front of the line. A finger on his shoulder and he turned, lost his place in line. Sharp teeth, heavy, sad eyes: Tely. Hipolit pointed absently over his shoulder, trying to communicate, and the vor wrapped his arm around Hipolit's neck and slipped him a loaf of prison bread.

"You don't stand in lines anymore. Not after tonight."

"The bandages are off."

"Good."

There was an excitability to the way Tely moved, a slight hunch in his neck suggested anticipation. The barracks buzzed with the same energy. They warmed their hands by a stove. Nine men in the room. They smoked and mumbled to each other. Sneering Russian that didn't flow in any way that made sense to Hipolit. The sentences congealed. The group spoke. Tely sat on a stool. He mumbled quickly. Hipolit heard suka several times. Tely unbuttoned the young man's shirt and the nine men nodded.

The zeks filed out. The adrenaline Hipolit had mainlined since his stunt at the mine tapered off. The bubble of silence crept up on him again, and he couldn't hear a thing. The sky was gray. A vor threw snow at another. Big laughs.

A guard approached them. Man with a purpose. Makarov wrapped in white knuckles. Everyone was quiet. The guard ignored his soaked pants. A skull screamed between his eyes.

His shoulder connected with Hipolit's, hard. The Pole spun to face him but he was already a yard away. Stomping. Oblivious. Hipolit shrugged.

They crept around the side of the schoolhouse and everything was silent. In the distance they heard two gunshots, close together. Then a third. They all turned at the sound, instinctually. Predatory.

Tely commanded their attention. They blinked and forgot the gunshots.

Point man cracked the door and stretched his neck inside. Shook his head and swung the door wide. They filed in. Hipolit waited in the snow. Looking in the direction of the gunshots. Tely motioned to him. Hopped up on chifir and vodka, a moment passed like a papercut, quick and painful. Promising more pain in the future.

Hipolit walked away.

He stopped and turned back but the schoolhouse door was closed. He felt for his heart in his armpit. He couldn't feel the beat. He turned around to go and almost ran face first into Alek Karriker.

"Going around shooting people?"

Hipolit showed him his hands.

"It's late, comrade."

Hipolit swallowed.

"Bread?"

Hipolit shook his head.

"Remember what I said about asking. You can ask. You didn't sneak into my place this time, which makes me happy. I'd be willing to negotiate."

Hipolit's eyes glazed. He shook his head again and squared his shoulder and passed the guard's bump onto Karriker.

Karriker brushed off his coat. "Don't hold a grudge."

Hipolit disappeared and Karriker hopped up the steps to his house.

Tely and the vors laid Karriker's options out for him: a shard of glass or a piece of sandpaper. His shadow covered the instruments as he leaned over to pick them up. The glass was a bit dull and he had trouble figuring how he'd be able to keep a grip on it once it broke the skin. The sandpaper would take longer. But, it wouldn't open any veins. He sank back onto his knees. The prisoners writhed in the darkness, he could hear them breathing heavy. Wetting their lips. The kerosene lamp swung above his head. Spotlight. Tely smiled his sharp teeth in the membraneous dark and Karriker clenched his jaw shut.

"Your arm says that you are a thief. This is a lie. Your hand says that you're a *great* thief. This is also a lie. Your fingers say your name but your name is false. Your fingers say your name is Alek. What is your real name?"

Karriker picked up the square of sandpaper.

"We know your real name. Suka. On your back, those towers mean nothing. Seven years? Seven years where?"

Karriker studied the sandpaper. "Where did you get this?"

"Across your stomach, you claim that you are a card maker, but this is—"

"A lie?"

"Indeed."

Karriker shrugged. Felt his neck heat up.

"You're a bitch and a traitor. Suka. We talk to Moscow. Do you talk to Moscow?"

"I don't."

"Moscow tells us that sukas are not to be suffered, anymore."

"There are many sukas in this camp."

"There will be many dead men."

"Shoot me."

"We will. In time. First, you kill the lie. You correct the untruths you've told us. Then you must live in the truth. Then, we shoot you."

Room dripped damp like a cellar. Yellow light burned red when Alek Karriker closed his eyes. His throat was sore. The walls pulsated with skin. Blurred green symbols stretching and arcing with every muscle twitch.

Deep breath.

He began to rub his forearm like he was scrubbing in the shower. The heat rose. The irritated skin glowed bright pink. White shavings of dead skin stuck in the hairs.

A red line extended from the cross-hatched grip of the Makarov, straight down into the snow and across the camp, and Ilya Bogrov walked it like a tight rope, riding the pulse of norepenephrine from point A to B, from the bloodless blue body, through the crowd of zeks, straight to Wu's cabin. The door exploded off its hinges and the small man looked up from his desk and at the gun in Bogrov's hand and he set his pen down and folded his arms over each other and asked him what he needed.

Bogrov squinted and shot Wu between the eyes, spraying his brains onto the wall behind him. Cordite killed the jasmine. Ink crept over the edge of the desk. Bogrov checked his pockets. Empty. The drawers kept papers and a bottle of vodka. Bogrov poured it out.

Brass and paktong lamps folded under his bootheel. Armfuls of teas and spices tumbled into the stove. Exacerbated by the flame, the spice smell once again conquered the room.

No opium.

He canvassed the room twice, and both times came up empty handed. On the third try he found a small bag inside a plush purple pillow. He wiped his mouth and tossed the bag into the flame.

Milena blinked and peeled her cheek off the floor.

After a short stint on her hands and knees she managed to stand. She got the door open in time to dry heave in the snow. The wind pinked her skin. Seconds into it she couldn't feel her fingertips.

She revived the dying fire in her stove. The warmth stung and got her teeth chattering.

Picking up the bottle from her desk, she poured the last sip of vodka down her throat.

Her room reeked.

She rallied a mop and bucket from her closet. Melted snow in the bucket and dipped the mop. The hard pink chunks of vomit from the night before pasteled under the water. The steadiness of the mopping got her synapses firing. She mopped the urine in the corner.

Reaching once again into her cleaning supply closet, she removed a ratty towel and a jug of ammonia, which she used to towel up the wet shit and dump over the dark stain, respectively. Tossed the towel outside.

She inspected her clothes, wrinkled from a night crumpled on the floor. Bodily fluid-free.

She paused for a moment in front of the door that led into the hospital. Straightened the lines in her shirt. Cinched up her pants.

Milena could not shake the dizziness. Nothing would stay in its place. Everything was on ice.

The door wouldn't open. She turned the knob as far as it would go and shoved it with her shoulder. It budged an inch. On her third push she heard something heavy fall away and the door swung open.

Blood, everywhere.

She returned to earth for a second and she closed her eyes. She tried to sober up but the room would not stop spinning.

Karriker's skin tapered off into the beaches of calm bloody lakes, a thin shiny patch where each tattoo had been. His hands were gnarled hunks of flesh. They'd rubbed the tattoos off of his back.

She lifted him onto an empty bed. She tripped and the legs of the cot screeched.

The patients watched.

She forced her fingers to roll the combination. Dosed him twice with morphine. Swabbed each wound thoroughly with iodine. Applied bandages. She stopped and puked on the floor. The sour smell mixed with the iodine and blood. The world turned and she fell forward, crossways over Karriker's body, and passed out.

Bogrov took his last two tablets of streptomycin. He didn't miss the hospital, but he didn't like running out of medicine. He alternated sleeping for a few hours and sitting in front of his wall, staring. Stretched the kinks out. Kneaded the bad leg. Sweat streamed over his stoic face. Spittle and grit teeth.

Stray pieces of straw littered the floor. Fourteen sticks of dynamite crammed the space under his mattress. He paced for a long time. Limping. Turning a bomb over in his hands.

The reveille rang in the cool morning air. A mob congealed quickly around Wu's barracks. Guards waved to disperse. The mob thinned. Two uniforms removed the Chinaman's body. The mob found a new point of interest: the armory. They crowded around the guardhouse. A soldier pushed his way through and made motions to disperse. They got one last look at the dead man's throat and scattered.

The reveille proceeded.

Back in his room, Bogrov stoked the fire. The dynamite warmed under the mattress, shaking off the subzero nitroglycerin freeze.

Bogrov hacked into his hand and wiped his mouth. The explosives slept in the supply shed for an eternity, but aged well. One plus to the arctic cold—no sweating. He coughed again.

Puke-heavy air in the chamber. Milena, ass in the air, passed out over a body mostly covered in bandages. Bogrov returned his empty pill bottle to his pocket and carried her into her office, sat her in her chair, and closed the door.

The mummy groaned. Blood soiled the bandages brown. The wrap peeled back like a second skin. Smell hit him hard. The prisoner said his name and he looked into his eyes.

Bogrov's hands trembled. He removed the bloody bandages. Cleared out a cabinet with a swoop of his arm, metal tools on the floor. A stack of clear white towels. He daubed the wounds and applied more iodine. None of the wounds were deep enough for stitches. Bogrov twirled the gauze. Virginal, timid fingers. Karriker screamed. Face streaming tears and sweat and snot.

Bogrov threw himself into a stool, forehead soaking. Karriker shook epileptic, shiny yellow teeth glinting in the hospital light.

They'd moved things around in Wu's shack, first the guards then the thieves. The pillows were gone, as was the bust of Stalin. Four ghostly circles the only reminder of the big oak desk. Still, that faint smell of jasmine. No one cleaned the brains off of the wall. Bogrov took a pick-axe to the floorboards. On the first swing the boards buckled. On the second the pick pierced through the wood and he leaned into the handle and an ugly chunk of wood came up.

Repeat.

He'd torn up half the floor when he found the stash, pounds and pounds of the powder tucked snugly into sheer plastic bags.

Tucking two ounces into his coat, he emptied his pockets on the floor. Blasting caps, two sticks of dynamite, matches. Shoving the cap firmly into soft middle, smell of sawdust in his nose, he did not tremble.

He sat back in the stool, breathing heavy. Smoke smeared on his face. Coughing black clouds. Set the white bundle on his friend's chest and opened it with his fingernails. Pinching the powder between his hands, he sprinkled the powder into Karriker's eager mouth. He watched him smile and ate a fingernail's worth and picked broken glass and splinters from his skin.

Their stomachs contracted around their respective rations of bread and the men fell heavy on their cots, the grit from the day's work grinding into the slick mold of their blankets. Hipolit took off his clothes and scratched the tattoo on his chest, white flakes of skin dancing like dust motes in the weak lamp glow. Voices drowned in the white light of his inner ear, and his head hit the pillow, so primed for sleep that it didn't come right away, mercifully prolonging his short moment of pleasure. He opened his eyes one last time and saw the dangling feet of his bunkmate, still in his boots. One of them was without a shoelace, much like the piecemeal shoes typical of the zek. But the other had a shoelace, that dangled in front of Hipolit, crusted with dirt but for the part stained darker than the earth.

The next time Karriker opened his eyes he saw nobody for a long time. His bed was surrounded by a sheet. He heard voices but did not know whose they were. He floated the nauseating tide of opiates and sunk to where the water got dark, but the sun poked through and he had to shield his eyes from the slightest rays. Had to go deeper.

Bogrov set a cigarette endwise on his stool.
A zek dried himself with a scabby towel.
Bogrov flipped open a pen knife.
The zek memorized the blade, every nick and shine.
Bogrov speared the knife into the head of the cigarette. He spun the end of the blade, twisting out shavings of tobacco. Having loosened the leaves in the paper, he rolled the paper between his palms until the cigarette became a mostly hollow tube.
The zek got dressed and left. Signaled to the next in line: the bath is free.
Bogrov waved the loose makhorka off the stool and dug in his pocket and sprinkled the powder into the empty cigarette.
A new zek undressed. He unsaddled the giant wooden cross from around his neck and laid it on the table next to the wash basin.
Bogrov lifted his trembling hand to his mouth and lit a match and made the end glow. He got something, but it wasn't right. His extremities warmed and his gums got numb but his brain was stubbornly cognizant.

The zek splashed and blubbered in the water like a child.

Bogrov put out the cigarette.

The zek drew his face from the basin and shook his head like a dog and smiled a row of shark teeth at Bogrov.

Bogrov looked at the dead cigarette on the ground and back at the bathing prisoner and then back at the cigarette.

The zek said "Something smells good in here," and Bogrov scooped his stuff into his pockets. Pulled his coat tight and threw the door open.

Smell of antiseptic. The hospital made him queasy. Bogrov rolled a cigarette for Karriker. He put too much opium in the paper and the cigarette fell apart. Karriker tried to keep his voice steady. His face turned red. Fingers trembled through the awkward husk of his bandages. His eyes burned into Bogrov's work, and Bogrov could feel the pressure, causing his own hands to shake, which once again ruined the cigarette. Karriker did not yell at him, instead jamming his finger into a small hole in his pillow and tearing.

The third try was a charm. Bogrov stuck the cigarette in Karriker's mouth and lit the tip until the opium vaporized. Karriker inhaled and the smoke curled around his face and got in his eyes and he coughed.

Once he was suitably high he stood up and walked around the room. Nothing was broken. He could still feel the pain through the veil of the drug, but he could move. His skin stretched and broke, the wounds reopened and he bled. He walked from one end of the room to the next, tiny circles of blood dripping behind him. The walls were breathing around him. He fought for space. The air was tight and close. He was a clay man left in the sun to dry. Flaking. The light hit the curtain and turned his vision blue like the sky that never showed its face over the camp. He kept walking and Bogrov kept smoking.

"We'll keep you high and you'll be fine."

Ilya Bogrov sat by Karriker's bed until he nodded off. His wandering mind snapped to attention when he heard the low hum like the voice of God coming from the cut in Karriker's throat.

Anton Nikitin's bones were sticks. His face lost all light. Rubber, a mask. The eyes lived somewhere else. His voice retained its timbre, giving the impression of a ventriloquist dummy. When Karriker finally decided to stop pretending to be asleep, Nikitin raised a gnarled hand that shook against gravity and laid it across Karriker's palm and suddenly he was a human again, and Karriker felt ashamed for thinking his friend was anything less and he hurt so bad he wanted to scream.

Nikitin's face looked perfectly human and he said, "It's going to get a lot worse before it gets any better."

The astringent in the soap had turned Tely's skin pink and made his face glow. He was almost good looking until he smiled, the pygmy teeth devouring all the light in the room, and Hipolit had learned to never trust a vory v zakone when he grinned. Tely especially.

They caught him on his trip home from the mine. Four of them pinned him to a wall, one for each limb. Tely took center stage. A large peninsula of acne streaked his cheek.

Hipolit wet his pants.

"It's like this. You've been marked, Hipolit. Your chest tells a story. The story makes claims on your person. On who you are. When you got that mark you agreed to a contract. Contracts are written in blood. Our contracts are permanent. There is a rule that you didn't follow and now you think you can just forget about it? Forget about the mark we've given you?"

He scratched the trench of pimples.

"It's fucked. It's all fucked. Moscow is not happy. The bosses are not happy. There's a war, Hipolit. You know. You signed the contract."

Hipolit caught his breath and stammered. "I can still help you."

Tely tapped his teeth. "I don't know."

"I know another suka we can find."

Tely poked out his chin and the four vors let Hipolit go. He fell on all fours and grabbed Tely's feet. "I'm sorry. I can help you. I'm sorry."

They crouched outside of Bogrov's apartment.

Hipolit talked fast. "He lives in there. He's like you, I've seen it. Under his cap, he has a tattoo. A screaming skull. But he's been a guard here for as long as I can recall. And he's always with the other suka, the one you killed."

"And you're sure that he's one of us?"

"Unless you know another reason a man would have a tattoo on his forehead."

Tely squinted at the cabin. Hipolit shifted his feet. "So, now I'm safe, right? I've helped you? I've earned the mark?"

Tely smiled. "Just leave." He turned to his comrades. "Which do you think it will be tonight, boys? The sandpaper or the knife?"

The night passed quietly. Bogrov sat in the middle of his room, staring at the wall. He touched his purpled eye. Tongued the recess where his teeth used to be. The gash on his forehead stopped bleeding after it ran its course. Flakes of scab floated like ash.

Five men lay dead around his room, faces contorted into varying degrees of fear and shock.

Bogrov lit an opium cigarette and wiped the dried blood off his knuckles.

Alek Karriker's throat sucked souls at night. The moon rose and he rocked back and forth in his bed, sweat beading and teeth gritting, and his throat opened from one end to the other and the light beamed, so thick it could shine through a human body, and his esophagus would flap out, and it would creep over the edge of the bed and slither along the floor, hacking and grunting. It would spiral up a bedpost and hang over another patient like an asp, and it slid up the nostril and down the throat and vacuumed up the soul. The victim died and the pools of Karriker's blood dried up.

During the day he slept.

Milena rolled the prisoners out into the cold and rolled empty beds in. They were filled, usually the same day, with new prisoners. Guards, sentries. Skin removed. Most died before nightfall, and the demon in Karriker's esophagus swallowed the rest.

Apraxin visited once. He didn't sit down. Knotted up his dirty gloves between his fingers. He scratched the edge of a sullen bruise ringing his eye.

Karriker opened his eyes.

The head of camp administration shrugged. Eyes glistened in the window light. "It's off, Alek."

Karriker's face remained stony.

Apraxin receded to the doorway.

The hospital kept its mouth shut.

Karriker walked heel to toe from one end of the room to the other. Bogrov leaned against the wall and clapped. The missing beds made the room bigger. Outside, Milena shouted at a man in a hospital gown, his knees knocking together, gesturing frantically toward the inside. Breath coming out in panicked train puffs. Milena forced him back with the point of her gun.

Karriker squatted. "So what do we do?"

Bogrov shrugged. "They're everywhere. Hundreds of them. I see them every day. Looking at me. Waiting for a chance to come at me again."

"It'll be soon."

"I know. For you, too."

Karriker took a cigarette from Bogrov's outstretched hand. "Yeah."

"I could kill them."

"Hundreds of them?"

"They're coming for us. We could hit them first."

Karriker stood up and paced. "Is the objective to live?"

Bogrov smoked. "Debatable."

"My vote goes for living. Hurting seems like a waste of our time."

"So where do we go?"

"West."

"A truck?"

"Road only goes to the mine."

"Train tracks?"

"Too easy for them to find us. It'd be what they'd expect."

"Through the woods, then."

"Yeah."

"You and me."

"We'll need more."

"I don't know anyone."

Karriker put out his cigarette. "I'll handle it."

Bogrov looked him over. "I've never seen anyone recover as fast as you. You have a shit diet. You have tuberculosis."

Karriker cupped a hand to the fogged window. Milena patrolled the freezing zeks. "Latest science from Moscow."

Persuasion

Nikitin sat on his stool. No book. Karriker outlined his plans. The guards made circles around them, holding their dogs at a length on their leash. The animals all pointed their noses at Nikitin and whined.

"You want to head west through the forest. Then over the tundra."

"Yes."

"Do you even know what town we're aiming for?"

"We're not aiming for towns. India, I was thinking."

"India."

"No one will look for us there."

"Alek, I'm old."

The wind beat their clothes. Karriker shuffled his feet. "You're not that old."

"No one will look for us anywhere. Apraxin's lost his mind."

"We'll get as far as we need to."

The old man meditated on that for a moment. "I'm in. We need to do this soon."

"I know."

"We'll need supplies. Food. As much bread as we can carry. Guns. Coats."

"We've got it all. Ilya raided the kitchen and the armory. Milena can strip the coats off her patients."

"Milena and the man with the tattoo. Are those the only others you're bringing?"

"Milena couldn't get out of here fast enough. She had

her bag packed before I was done talking."

"Yes, but are these the only others?"

Karriker paused. "Yes."

Nikitin sunk deeper into his chair. "You haven't thought this through well enough, I'm afraid."

"What do you mean?"

"If we have a gun, I can shoot deer. That's as far as the forest, though. Once the woods run out, to the west and south, it's kilometers and kilometers of tundra. Weeks worth. No matter how much deer meat we pack, we'll run out. Bread, too. And then what? And then how fast do you think the cold will finish us?"

The two of them sat in the quiet for a long time. "So what do we do?"

Nikitin rubbed his temples. "We need a calf."

Karriker mimicked Nikitin's posture. "God."

"I know."

Sighing through his nose, Karriker said, "Well, who?"

They watched guards pass for fifteen minutes.

Nikitin pointed them out. "See him, he's too big. There'd be plenty of meat, but he'd put up a fight. We're all going to be exhausted, here, we can't afford for any of us to be hurt. And him, over there, he's just bones. No sustenance."

"Not to mention every single one of these men would either run to the vory v zakone or Apraxin as soon as they heard our plan."

Nikitin's eyes lit up. "I know someone who wouldn't."

Hipolit tried to avoid the old man, but he'd been made, and when Nikitin approached him he winced reflexively and asked him what he wanted.

"Do you remember when I stopped you from leaving?"

The Pole's hands migrated south, away from his face. "I do."

"What if I told you I made a mistake?"

"I'd tell you that you were right."

"What if I told you I wanted to make it right?"

Hipolit swept the perimeter for prying ears. "I'd wonder if you didn't work for Apraxin. I'd wonder if you weren't trying to get me to say something."

"Why wouldn't I have just turned you in when I caught you the first time?"

"People change. Minds change."

"I'm old. My mind hasn't changed since before you were born."

Hipolit bounced on his toes. "Okay, fine. I don't care if you turn me in. What's the plan?"

Nikitin smiled and looked over his shoulder. "You hear that boys? We've got a zek here that wants out."

The Pole's eyes narrowed. "I *knew* it!"

The old man laughed. "Calm down. That was a joke."

Hipolit forced himself to stop shaking, then squeezed out a laugh. "Seriously, though. What's the plan?"

"Four of us are getting out of here, tomorrow night. We need a fifth man."

"Why? Wouldn't that just split the rations even more?"

"Not if you pull your weight and bring food along. It'll keep us all alive longer."

Hipolit tried to work the math in his head and failed.

"Where are you going?"

"India."

"The fuck would I do in India?"

119

"Work in a mine would be my guess, son. I don't care what you do in India. If you like Siberia so much, then I'm sorry, I've got the wrong man."

Hipolit paddled in the middle of the ocean, his limbs getting tired and the sharks circling, and he had a choice: climb on the driftwood that's caught on fire or drown. Or get eaten.

He put his hand on the fire. "I'm in. Tomorrow night?"

"Meet at the sally port. Be discreet."

Hipolit nodded. "I'll be there."

Back at sea, he curled into a ball on the slick driftwood and fell asleep to the smell of burning flesh.

The last quarter of his cigarette dying a smoky blue death on the metal table next to his cot, Alek Karriker dreamed of revenge. He'd been back to the schoolhouse earlier that day. The bed was torn to shreds. The stove was knocked over. Paint splashed everywhere. His desk was pulp. It would be swept, the splotchy paint and chalk writing painted over, and new beds would be moved in and the new recruits would be told nothing of the room's history, which if they were lucky wouldn't repeat itself.

The dream came peaceful at first. He walked the streets of New Delhi barefoot. He visited the Taj Mahal and met brown skinned girls that he'd never tell Milena about. He wandered the markets and bought ornate rugs on the cheap. The sun voided the need for shirts. His skin was mottled, too pink in some areas and a reflective white in the others, but the citizens of India still thought him beautiful and unique. Buying an apple from a vendor outside of a bank, he had the occasion to meet the man's gaze, which turned to a spot above his right shoulder. He craned his neck in the direction the vendor was looking and noticed that in his right hand he held a stick, and attached to the end of that stick was the head of Hipolit the Pole, and he bought another apple from the man and fed it to the jawing face above him.

He was naked in his dream, and when he woke up his hands flailed for the pike. Memories flooded in, and he remembered his conversation with the Pole, just outside his door, just before the attack. He owed Nikitin for this one. He would pay him back.

Hipolit's flesh was going to taste sweet.

The tattooed men closed in like a vice. Cats and skulls and wolves. Ilya Bogrov saw them milling around his barracks, waiting for him to come home. They crawled over the bath shack. They slithered about the train station. Some of them held their shanks in the open. Some pretended to shave.

Bogrov kept his head down and booked to the hospital. Footsteps echoing, every bed empty except for Karriker's. His friend slept hard. Milena reclined in a stool in front of the door to her office, a Kalashnikov curled in her lap.

Bogrov slumped into a cot. "Where did you hide them?"

She stepped lithely from her stool and disappeared into her office. When she came back she had a twin gun extended butt-first. Bogrov made sure it was loaded. Cocked.

A half-empty bottle of vodka caught his eye. His chest burned at the thought of drinking that much.

Milena smiled at him. "Did you want some?"

Bogrov touched his stomach involuntarily. "No."

121

She didn't mind. In an hour she emptied the bottle and listened to the tone of it clinking against her rifle. She was still in uniform. Neither of them spoke.

"You're not Alek's friend."

Bogrov shrugged.

"I know about what you do. When you take the men out. Make it look like escape. And now you're escaping. You really are escaping."

Bogrov laid back in the bed.

"It's funny, kind of funny. In the way it's funny when God takes something away from you. Or funny like this place is funny."

"Funny like freezing your patients."

Milena threw the bottle at Bogrov's head. It burst on the wall. "I have to do that. It's the—"

"The latest science from Moscow, I know. I have heard."

"I don't have a choice."

"It's funny."

Milena crossed her arms.

Bogrov looked down the barrel of his gun. "I don't know who I am. I wake up. Look in the mirror. There are things I do that make me a certain way." His throat dried. "I loved being a soldier. Rules. I liked it. I've never made an excuse in my life. But this place is full of rats. You have to be like a rat. And I didn't know this, and I paid for it."

Milena's head drooped. Big snore like a motor.

Bogrov didn't say anything for a long time.

At the morning reveille Apraxin made an announcement. There would be a new division in the camp devoted to the manufacture of skis. He rattled off a list of names and those chosen thanked God and made their way to the schoolhouse.

Hipolit piled into the truck bound for the mine. On any other day, the news would have bothered him. Not being chosen would have bothered him. But not today. Not on his last day in camp 117.

He barely swung the pick at all, only once or twice when the foreman walked by. No sense in leaving the camp with cracked ribs. He talked to a couple of the zeks working close to him, none of whom answered. No offense taken. He thought about his friends in Warsaw, and his friends in Moscow. Thought about the *stilyagi,* the stylish ones. Big clown shoes and Elvis hair. Chewed paraffin in lieu of gum. Pictured a girl with red hair and red lips.

The day ended.

The prisoner in front of him took the bucket up and Hipolit remembered the girl he lost, the same as he did every day. Being pulled from his doors by the *Kommisarat,* the young lieutenant holding her gently and cupping her mouth as they dragged Hipolit away, the door shutting and his stomach and chest heaving. The screaming he did in the back of the truck. All of it close, in his face.

He could smell her hair and he could smell the communal showers of his apartment complex, he could feel the lukewarm water he'd once hated. He could feel that hair when it was wet. He could see her blue eyes.

He remembered the train ride to camp, the boxcar so thick with men that no one could lift their hands from their sides. The wind so deadly that the men along the outer wall began to freeze, and soon a consensus was reached, that the prisoners would rotate out from the warm center of the car every hour. Making sleep impossible. He had been unable to breathe since that train ride, and now he finally felt his lungs expand, taking in the chalky air of the mineshaft.

He stepped into the bucket and looked up at the faint, fading light at the top. The rope creaked. He fingered the tattoo through his shirt. He wondered what she'd think. He wondered if she'd laugh.

The bucket birthed into the light and Hipolit swung his foot to the landing. Someone yelled and he heard a terrible twisting, snapping sound and felt the solid ground of the bucket drop from below his foot. He plummeted down the mineshaft, pinballing off the sides, crumpling into a heap of broken bones.

The last thing he saw before he died were the curious, dirty faces of his coworkers, each one of them thanking God that it was him and not them.

Nikitin planted the dynamite under the support structure of Apraxin's office. The dying sun flung pinks and yellows into the sky and the prisoners were headed for their daily rations and Anton Nikitin could hear the weepy sounds of the sonata coming through the walls in his boss's house. Nikitin sneered at the hypocrisy. His boss, for all his Muscovite ass-kissing, was a pirate, listening to illegally x-rayed vinyl data off of nondescript metal plates.

Everyone had their vices.

Nikitin inserted the blasting caps and twirled wire around the ends of each. The wire met in a neat little knot at his feet, which he lit with end of a cigarette.

Hobbling as quickly as he could, the music ended with the exhale of flame, the heat on his back so foreign to his skin that he broke out in hives.

The distraction worked. The mob swarmed, both the tattooed and the clear-skinned gathered shoulder to shoulder to watch Apraxin and his cabin burn. Bogrov, Milena and Karriker slipped out the back of her hospital into the courtyard. They hopped the fence.

The old man waited for them in the sally port. The four of them thumbed the straps of their knapsacks. They all smelled like yeast and gun lubricant. Hundreds of voices mumbled in the distance.

Karriker laced his fingers at the base of his neck. "Where is this fucker?"

Nikitin checked his watch. "I don't know, Alek, but if he doesn't show soon we're going to have to leave anyway."

Karriker bit his lip. Swept the ushanka off his head and stomped it. "Fuck."

Bogrov and Milena stood at the end of the sally port, their eyes unable to stay still, glancing out into freedom and back at their comrade, cursing his hat.

Nikitin picked it out of the snow and brushed it off. "Come on. He figured it out. Or maybe he just changed his mind. Maybe he's dead."

Karriker shook his head. "He's not dead, that little fucker. That *fucker*."

"Alek—"

"He's just *staying*? After everything that's happened. He'd rather stay there than risk leaving? Fucking *coward*."

"Quit fucking around," Nikitin's voice dropped an octave. "Get it together and let's go."

The fire crackled in the distance. The voices seemed quieter, less concentrated.

Karriker nodded and put on his ushanka. He left the camp with his three comrades, but not without looking back to curse Hipolit's name one last time.

Karriker never smelled so much pine in his life. The first night they slept in a clearing a couple kilometers outside of camp, confident that no one would look for them until morning. If they even noticed they were gone.

"No one will notice me," Nikitin said, palms out toward the fire. "And neither will they miss Ilya or Alek. The vors might, but they won't notice for a time. With any luck the authorities will assume that Milena went up with the cabin."

Milena tore into her stale bread. "They'd think I was fucking Apraxin?"

"We can only hope."

Milena put her bread away.

Bogrov sat ramrod straight and said nothing the entire night. He only moved when Karriker pinched a bit of opium from his knapsack and sprinkled it in his mouth. Karriker offered Bogrov the bag and his friend took a pinch for himself.

Few words passed between the group. The dilemma rested on the tip of everyone's tongue, where they let it sleep, praying that one of the other would die before it had to be brought up.

The first day's hike through the woods tried their stamina. Snowdrifts up to their knees put a burn into their thighs, but they continued on. At night they built a snowdrift to block the wind and Nikitin wandered into the woods to fetch kindling. Once the fire started they ate their bread.

All four of them took streptomycin daily from Milena's pouch.

"This is what I would use to make the reds on those cards."

Nikitin nodded. "I always figured. I knew it couldn't have been blood."

"Blood dries brown."

"Indeed it does. Your reds were brilliant. Maybe that's what you can do when we get to India."

"I'm sure the Indians have plenty of card makers. I'd be outmatched."

Nikitin rolled his blanket into a pillow. "Stop talking nonsense and go to sleep."

The second night, overcome with simple human need, Milena and Karriker attempted to make love while the other two slept. Karriker straightened out the bunches in the blanket and let her lay the closest to the fire. She bit into the thick of her palm and focused on not getting burned.

The third night they did it again, not even noticing that Bogrov slipped off into the darkness, only to reappear once they were finished. Milena ate two rations of bread.

That was the last time they touched each other.

Nikitin sighted down the barrel of the Kalashnikov. The rifle bucked against his shoulder and birds abandoned their perches in the canopy. The brown form in the distance folded against space.

They watched Nikitin clean the reindeer. Karriker looked into its black eyes and felt his throat become warm. Nikitin slit open the buck's stomach and Karriker looked away.

Nikitin turned the meat on the spit and talked.

"It would be good if we could have Tatyana with us. She was a fantastic tracker. I hoped that as we walked she would pick up my scent and join us. But, her pull to be a wolf is instinctual. There's really nothing I can do about it."

Karriker bit his thumb. Milena ate a ration of bread.

"It's a good thing she isn't male, because let me tell you, she'd probably already be the leader of whatever pack she's in!"

Karriker cleared his throat. "Anton, Tatyana is dead."

The old man stopped turning the spit. "What?"

"She's gone."

He smiled. "Nonsense, Aleksy. I've heard from her. She sent me a transmission."

"I saw her body. In the grave outside of camp."

"Must have been another dog."

"Tatyana was hard to mistake."

The forest did not make a sound. "Did she look hurt?"

"Not that I could see. She was an old dog, Anton."

"She sent me a transmission."

Everyone was quiet for a long time.

Karriker's gums bled on his bread. Crumbs like dry copper down his throat. The day closed its eyes. The fire blazed. He dropped the hunk of bread back into his deflated pack. When he closed it the phantom smell of deer meat crept into his nostrils. Bogrov smelled it too, and the two men commiserated in a glance.

Milena cauterized a hole in her boot. She drank vodka and did not eat.

Karriker sat next to her. "Are you out?"

She nodded.

Karriker sighed and opened his pack. He held the ration out to her. She thumbed the blood soaked into the yeast. And then she ate it.

Nikitin crossed his legs. "It's been several days since we've seen a reindeer."

Bogrov rotated a cigarette. "What about rabbits? Can you track rabbits?"

Karriker noticed a ring of black spots peppering the sliver of skin between Nikitin's boot and pant leg. The old man said, "There aren't any that I've seen. No tracks, either. If they are out here, they've probably burrowed."

"Well, can you spot a burrow?"

"If we come across one, sure. But like I said, there aren't any tracks to lead me there."

"Do we have any idea where we are?"

"I'm guessing about two hundred kilometers from camp."

Karriker cradled his head in his hands. "We're not even close to being out of it."

The old man adjusted his pant leg. "That's true. Probably halfway."

Milena took a sip. "We knew this was going to happen. That's why we were bringing that little Polish boy."

Karriker ran through a string of curses under his breath. Tried to force his brain to think.

Bogrov lit his cigarette. "We're not starving, yet."

Milena said, "By this time tomorrow, we will be."

Karriker held up a hand. "No, by this time tomorrow, we'll be hungry. We've been hungry before. We've spent our lives for the past few years hungry. We can hold out for a few more days." He pulled at the itchy dampness of his pant leg. "We've been walking in straight lines. Tomorrow we spread out. At least fifty meters apart, each. And we look for a burrow."

The night said nothing. Not a bird call or a wolf howl. Only the wind in the thinning pine. Longer stretches of the land were flat and white. Their camp crouched close to a rare grouping of trees. No one slept, and everybody watched everybody else.

The next day the forest thinned even more. The ground became barren but for random patches of scrub.

Past noon Nikitin found something. Tracks in the snow. The group rallied at the tracks and followed them a kilometer to the west. Once the tracks reached the burrow, they became lost in a labyrinthine tangle of different rabbit tracks. The four of them stared into the dark earth for a long time.

"Should we smoke it out?" Milena said.

Nikitin shook his head. "The smoke could asphyxiate it before it could escape. Then we'd just have a dead rabbit deep in a narrow hole."

They decided to move themselves back so as not to frighten whatever might be inside. Nikitin crouched against a skinny pine and brought the rifle up to his cheek.

The four of them barely breathed.

After an hour, Bogrov whispered what everyone was thinking. "There's no telling if the rabbit's even there. We could be wasting our time."

"We might as well smoke it out," Milena said.

The old man's voice got sharp. "We're not wasting the matches. If you think you can make it through the night without fire, then be my guest."

Another hour passed. Bogrov said, "We're wasting our

time. The longer we stay in the dead zone, the longer we starve. There's nothing here. We need to go."

They all stared longingly at the hole. Karriker said, "Milena's right. We should smoke it out."

Milena collected kindling. They set it at the base of the hole and Nikitin unearthed a page of *Pravda* from his pack and shredded it and set it on fire. The kindling didn't catch.

He sighed. "You see what we're doing? We're wasting our time and supplies."

Bogrov's eyes turned cold. "It would be in all of our best interest to get this rabbit, old man."

Nikitin wet his lips. He lit another piece of paper and set it across the sticks. On his hands and knees, he puffed at the fire and waved his hands. Thick black smoke plumed into the sky. He shoved the stick down the burrow, smoke roiling out in ugly gulps.

Three minutes passed without the sight of a rabbit.

After ten minutes, they decided to leave.

Karriker's throat hummed as they slept. It cracked open like a door after an ice storm, and the throat emerged, shivering against the cold.

The parasite in Alek Karriker needed a soul. The host weakened.

The pink rope slid blindly across the dirt, twisting left and right, looking for a warm body to violate. It felt a close presence. A young soul. Vibrant, but wounded. Easy to take and delicious. The warmth spread up the length of the throat to its base at the hinge of Karriker's spine. The heat grew greater and greater and the parasite readied itself for a soul.

The throat snaked into the open fire. It couldn't make a noise, but its silent scream snapped open Karriker's eyes. The throat retreated to its hole and Karriker's neck closed.

He hyperventilated and dry heaved in the snow. His esophagus burned.

The rest of group slept till dawn, exhausted from another day without food.

Three days later, Bogrov ate tree bark. Milena talked to something on her shoulder that no one else could see. Karriker chewed on a strip of his shirt.

Anton Nikitin hissed at Karriker who waved to Milena, who flagged down Bogrov. They convened around the spot where the old man was standing.

"Reindeer tracks," he said.

They worshipped. They knelt and felt the curves and the depth of the tracks. Bogrov paced like if he stood at the right spot he'd be able to see the deer from there.

The tracks followed a straight line across the plain. Their sore muscles flexed with adrenaline, their metabolism waking into life and eating away at their flesh.

Slate gray sky pushed down. They hunkered and charged. They followed their noses and uncovered dung still steaming in the arctic cold.

Three hours later they found it.

The reindeer ate scrub in a clearing like an asteroid crater. Nikitin laid on his stomach. The other three dropped. He squinted down his sight. The wind blew thin wisps of gray into his eyes.

Bogrov pressed his knife point into his own yellowed skin. He drooled. They all wiped away spit.

Nikitin said, "I have to get closer."

"Whatever you do," Bogrov said. "Do not spook it."

Nikitin didn't answer him. He wormed over the ice for twenty meters. He stopped and pressed his cheek on the rifle stock.

The three held their breath.

The reindeer lifted his head and sniffed the air. Turned to face them.

Nikitin cocked his rifle.

The deer flailed. Heavy hooves on the tundra.

Anton Nikitin squeezed the trigger.

The fire sprang to life. Nikitin leaned back against a log and sighed. "At least I'm good for something, right?"

The joke dropped dead weight onto his comrades' ears.

The old man dropped the façade. "I don't care what you think you're going to do. I'm the most capable member of this group. Who will make your fires? Who will hunt your food?"

Bogrov leaned close to the fire, resembling something from a dark bolgia. "Old man...*you* can't hunt our food for us."

Nikitin tried to swallow.

"That was your job. When you took aim at that deer, your life was on the line. If you didn't know that, you should have. We're not all going to starve out here."

"I can make—"

Milena interrupted. "I can make a fire. *Alek* can make a fire."

Karriker kept his mouth shut.

"You can't do this."

"Why not?" Bogrov ground his teeth. "It was your idea in the first place."

"This wasn't my idea."

"You had no problem putting up the Polack as a calf."

Karriker said, "We're not eating Anton."

"You'd rather die?"

"I'd die before I ate Anton."

Bogrov turned back to the old man. "Alek refuses. What about him, old man? Shall we kill him?"

Nikitin swiveled his head back and forth between the two groups. He shook his head. "I'm not eating Alek."

The old man scooped snow into a pot and held it to boil over the stove. After a minute his arm shook and he switched hands. The water bubbled and he poured it into the group's cups.

Bogrov sipped. "Who do you know the best, Alek?"

"What do you mean?"

"Out of the three of us, who would you say is your favorite?"

"This is the most I've ever heard you say."

"Which one?"

"I don't have one."

"You don't have one."

"I'm like a mother. I can't pick one of my children."

"One of your children is nearly eighty years old."

Nikitin cleared his throat. "I'm fifty-seven."

Bogrov mouthed the word "old." Then he said. "So which one of us is the one you'd miss the least?"

Karriker didn't say anything.

Bogrov pointed at Nikitin. "He's the father figure." And at Milena, "And she's the girlfriend. I'm just a guy you've known for, what…a month? Two months? You'd eat me. If you had to choose, you'd eat me."

"If I had to choose I'd eat the Polack."

"But the Polack's not here. Fuck. Who thought he'd be the smartest out of all of us?"

"I'm not eating anybody."

Milena said, "I'm going to eat something."

Bogrov said, "She beats you."

Milena's mouth made an O. "I don't *beat* him."

Nikitin nodded. "It's true. I've seen the bruises. I've seen them after they fight."

Bogrov laced his fingers. "Let's be frank about this, Karriker. Milena has had sex with you. Milena has beaten you. But you can find a new woman. In India, do you know what those women do to men with white skin?"

"I liked you better when you were silent."

"They will do things to you that you can only imagine. And let's say you two live together for the rest of your earthly lives. How long is that really going to be, with how much she drinks?"

Milena balled a fist.

"I'm not going to eat anybody."

"I'm just being utilitarian, here. I'm saying who is going to be the most useful to you?"

"Why do you care what I think?"

"Because anyone here will pounce on anyone else, the first chance they get. You're the only one who's not playing."

"I'm not eating anybody."

"We've established that Milena's usefulness is questionable. Very probably she's a negative for you, comrade. I will never have sex with you, that much is true. But I will never hurt you, either. You have a brain, Karriker. You were going to run that shop in the camp. You're smart. But being smart isn't enough. Because you'll have to do difficult things, and that's where I come in. I can help you to get these things done. There are things I'm good at, I think. Sometimes. I want you to picture yourself behind a big desk. I want you to picture," Bogrov's hands grabbed at nothing, his imagination struggling to conjure an image, "someone wretched being led through the door, to the chair in front of your desk. This man is helpless. His entire family is starving. He's going to be thrown on the streets. All because a band of thieves is stealing all of his profits. Now, I want you to picture me at your right side. Picture yourself nodding. Now, picture me being unleashed, set out into the world to right this wrong. I come back and I wipe my hands and the man thanks you and you nod from behind your desk. You give him bread. I'm telling you what your life could be."

"The more you talk the more I think we should just eat you."

Bogrov showed his teeth. "You can try. I want you to be with me in this decision, Alek. I don't want to have to kill you. I'm afraid. I'm afraid if I try to kill the old man you'll get in my way, maybe try to kill me. We don't need two dead bodies. I'd hate to eat you."

"I'm not eating anybody." He moved next to Nikitin. "We'll sleep in shifts."

"What will you do with him when you reach India? Read books all day? Sit and watch the world? Or her? What will you do? Cower and pray for liver failure?"

"We're sleeping in shifts." Nikitin handed Karriker his rifle. "Please. Let's just…get out of this with our heads."

Bogrov didn't say anything else. He sat cross-legged. Milena curled up next to the fire.

Karriker watched them sleep. Nikitin snored lightly

next to him. The walls of his stomach pressed together. The night held on for dear life. Ghost taste of deer in his mouth. His energy vented through the slit in his neck. His eyes closed.

He awoke to pressure on his chest. Milena's knees dug into his shoulders. He struggled and flopped like a fish. All he could see was her face, her ravenous eyes. His fingers flexed against silt and permafrost. He could hear it all. He heard Nikitin crying and begging. He heard the knife enter something soft over and over again. He heard the old man gurgle and choke on blood. He cursed Milena and bucked against her and spit in her face.

Alek Karriker settled into the snow a hundred meters from his comrades. He looked up at the trees stretching to a vanishing point. Intricate flakes twirled and melted on his skeletal visage. He held a pack in each hand, and brought Nikitin's to his chest. He unzipped it and reached inside. Novels. He flipped through each one, smoothing the dog-eared pages and reading the notes in the margins. He buried them under snow and laid back until he couldn't feel his fingers.

Bogrov fish-wrapped the meat in newspaper. He took the liver and the heart and the lungs. He stomped on the old man's head until he heard a crunch, then tipped the body over and let the brains out onto the paper like the yolk of an egg.

He cut meat from the buttocks, the legs. The tongue. Milena stood back, her hand over her mouth. When he was done sawing he started a fire and put the brains in the pot.

The two of them ate with their fingers. Milena wretched. Choked it down. Bogrov chewed with his mouth closed.

Karriker pushed himself out of the snow and walked back to the fire. Bogrov slept soundly. Milena's indulgent eyes glared up at him. He sat down and warmed his hands. She held the meat out to him and he pushed it away.

"Eat it."

He slapped the charred flesh out of her hands and hit her in the face. She fell heavy in the snow. Bogrov had woken a moment earlier. He reached into his pack and pulled out a handful of opium. He held it out to Karriker.

Karriker knocked his hand away and tried to repeat what he'd done to Milena. Bogrov's foot met his balls and crushed his dream.

"You don't have to eat and you don't have to smoke, but you're going to be calm."

The pain hammered at his kidneys. Milena, recovered from her attack, kicked him the ribs.

Burning with prominence in his mind's eye, Karriker's fingers probed the ground for his gun. It had to be there, somewhere. He felt the smooth wood of the Kalashnikov's stock. It was impossibly light. He brought it to his face and felt a scream of frustration in his belly.

"I dismantled that one. Didn't see how we needed three, anymore."

Karriker threw the useless piece into the snow and howled.

They spent the entire day at the same camp. Bogrov and Milena ate all day, and by the time the sun set they had eaten half of Nikitin's corpse. The fetid stench gagged them all at least once.

Several times Milena tried to get Karriker to eat. She pinned him down like she had the night before, with renewed strength brought on by the protein, and tried to pry his jaw open. Even after the will had been sapped from his arms and legs, Karriker managed to keep his mouth shut, lips smeared with blood and black char.

She threw the meat at his face. "Just die, then."

Karriker cried into his palms. Thick ropes of snot evacuated his sinuses. He threw the meat as far as he could and crawled on his hands and knees to where Milena sat. He put his head in her lap and she pushed him away.

The stars in his eyes radiated the most beautiful purples and blues that he'd ever seen. He felt a whiteness like cotton at the edges of his vision and he felt alone. The greatness of the universe oppressed him and he didn't want to die by himself, in the middle of nowhere.

With the last of his strength he laid back in Milena's lap. She crossed her arms and turned her head but did not force him away. Soon, despite herself, she began to pet his stubbled skull.

Karriker saw the dragon undulating in the sky, felt as though his whole body had fallen asleep, millions of ant-like pinpricks all over his being. He heard its breath and it was like standing at the edge of a volcano, the sky a twirling vortex of molten lava, and he felt the buzz of the purple coffin lights and shut his eyes.

Milena held him. Reacting to a strange impulse that she didn't understand, she took a razor from her pack and began to shave concentric circles into Karriker's hair.

As they slept the parasite woke in Karriker's throat. It sensed danger. Death. The host had hardly any life left. Time had come that the parasite had to break the rules. They were close enough. The throat split open and the pink demon raised up into the night. Karriker's body rose with it, hands and legs limp and sliding against the snow. The back of his skull pressed firmly into his spine, Alek Karriker's body began to float through the trees and into the black void of the Siberian tundra.

When Milena and Bogrov awoke, they could not find Karriker's body. They packed their belongings and ate breakfast and set out, continuing their southward course to India.

The parasite brought him home. The place he'd been meant for. Hundreds of kilometers across tundra, at the base of the Himalayan mountains. The floating body waited. Ice crusted on the dry pastel of his esophagus.

Two figures materialized in the blizzard. One tall, one short. Both of their heads, open like cans. Throats out like periscopes. The three creatures hummed at each other, speaking in a language based on tones. The bodies hung limp.

The sentries approved of Karriker's presence. They guided his parasite up the mountain, along treacherous ravines and under drifts of snow primed and waiting for an avalanche. They took him deep into a valley surrounded on both sides by sheer walls of ice.

The valley was teeming with activity. On each of the ice walls there was a passageway, and through it there was a constant string of women. They moved, glassy eyed, from one to the other, all of them cradling afterbirth in their hands.

Makeshift carts and shops lined the smooth street between the giant doors. Men and women yelled frantically at the zombified women, trying desperately to get their attention. The women would occasionally stop at a storefront, the shop window lined with fine silks and cotton, and they would slip a coat or a shawl or a shirt onto their placenta, and they would continue on, until they found the cloth that fit it perfectly.

The throat rolled back into its home and Karriker opened his eyes. He wandered among the throngs of women, doing his best to talk to them, trying to understand why they were there. Trying to figure out why *he* was there.

He heard a voice shouting at him from one of the shops and he ran over. A squat man covered in warts motioned for him to come inside. A fire blazed in the hearth. Columns of cloth lay against the walls, scissors and sewing machines littered the floor.

The squat man brought him a steaming plate of corn and squash. Karriker finished it before his host could sit down.

"So you passed," the squat man said.

"Passed what?"

"The auditions."

"I didn't realize I was auditioning for anything."

"None of us ever really did. They're sneaky about it. They send us the animals, we don't know why."

Karriker asked for another plate. The squat man laughed and obliged.

"The animals. The empty animals?"

"With just the placenta, yeah. Course, it's not really *our* auditions. The demons, they do all the work."

"Demons."

141

"It's what I think they are. You ask anyone around here, they'll all give you different answers. Some of them think it's the tribes out here."

"Tribes? The Inuits?"

"Nah, probably not them."

"Then who?"

"No one really knows. But they provide a service. It's a good one, sure."

"Service?"

"We're retailers, son."

"What is it that we're selling?"

"Life."

Karriker asked for more food.

"The bands of people around here, they have interesting thoughts. Regarding life." The squat man turned a pair of scissors over in his hand. "The women out there, they aren't...real. Exactly."

"Looked real."

"Well, they are. I guess."

"You aren't Russian."

"Me? Nah. American."

"I can understand you."

"Yeah, we can all understand each other. Life's wonders."

Karriker set his plate down and rubbed his stomach. "I don't feel afraid."

"Me neither. Haven't since I got here."

"So what do I do now?"

"They'll set you up with a place. A shop or maybe just one of those numbers on wheels. You'll sleep and the demon will make its clothes. You wake up and you sell 'em."

"Where do the women come from?"

"It's just their souls. We exist…outside of time, or in a slowed down version of time. Something. The women, when they give birth, their souls come here. People out here say the placenta is the child's protector. Some of the tribes even make a crib for the thing. Maybe there's a mountain pass for that, too. But the women here are just shopping for clothes. Clothes for their baby's protector."

Karriker looked out the window at the women passing, staring blankly, taking pieces of cloth down from the shop windows and shaking them out and slipping their husks of flesh into them.

Karriker nodded. "I'm dead. This is hell."

The squat American shook his head. "No. If you fail to sell your wares, you get to leave. The demon though, how it chooses to exit your body…I've seen them go quietly, and not so quietly. I'd as soon not take the risk. Plus," he grinned big yellow teeth. "I'm a hell of a salesman."

Several years later Karriker wondered how exactly the demon would exit his body. The clothes were not selling. The American was right, he *was* a hell of a salesman, and Karriker was unlucky enough to be set up right next to him. The women crowded around his shop all day long, struggling for a chance to look at his wares.

He'd go to sleep and when he woke up only a few shirts, usually gray or black, would be waiting for him. The parasitic demon inside his throat had lost its inspiration.

On the day before he made his knee-quaking journey to The Boss, he'd been just about ready to pack up shop when a woman approached his display window. He'd gone through his sales pitch without even looking at her, his voice monotone and tired. She picked one of the gray

143

shirts off of the rack and fit the placenta inside.

This level of interest was unusual. Karriker looked up and almost fell over.

Milena took the placenta out of the outfit and put on another.

Karriker grasped for words. "How are you? Where are you? Where did you go? What happened to Ilya?"

But the women's souls were not capable of communication. She took her placenta under her arm.

"Wait wait wait. Who's the father?"

Milena walked away.

"Who's the father?"

She paid for a garment from the American's booth.

"Where are you? How can I find you?"

She disappeared into the hole in the mountain. Karriker held his head in his hands and closed his shop for the last time.

Of Icy Death and Human Folly

An Afterword
by Jeremy Robert Johnson

The Siberian tundra is a *motherfucker*. When Stalin's buddies at the GULAG agency positioned their slave labor camps it was the tundra which ensured, even more than the great-white-shark-infested waters surrounding Alcatraz, that escape was a joke.

Oh, you made it past the guards and the fence?

Good for you. Hope you can subsist on icy rocks and winds that'll freeze-dry your sorry skin in less than an hour. And you may want to stay very quiet in tiger territory. They'll be hungry like you.

So when J. David Osborne told me he was working on a book set in a Siberian Gulag he already had my interest. It's a setting that screams high conflict: man vs. nature, man vs. man, man vs. self....

Then, when he explained the concept of the fatted "calf" that acted as mid-tundra sustenance, he had not only my interest but my bated breath. This was a book I wanted to read, and NOW. It became my favorite future Swallowdown title to describe to people.

Two years later, the file landed in my inbox. I was expecting a great read. But what I didn't expect was for the damn thing to be one of the most audaciously sure-footed, mind-bending, prodigious opening acts since DFW's <u>The Broom of the System</u>. The economy and precision of language, the rich historical detail blended with decidedly surreal grace-notes, the multi-character narrative tied into the central arc, the Russian nesting doll metaphor of prisons within prisons within prisons (within prisons), the sort of lovely Vonnegut "So It Goes" sigh underlying the hard-boiled style...

This book is a *motherfucker*. Like <u>Catch-22</u> as adapted for film by David Lynch. And I got to read it first. I love my job.

Now I'm passing this beast to you Dear Readers, with a nice Russian mini-glossary popped in there and an *amazing* cover from the outstanding Alex Pardee (and a great portrait of Our Hero Alek Karriker from pen-and-ink ace Erin Elise). I sincerely hope you enjoy this ripping read as much as I did.

On a side note—Folks have been asking for the submissions guidelines for Swallowdown Press. There are none; I'm only taking solicited manuscripts. I'm scouting. I'm hunting for work that presses my buttons. I found Cody Goodfellow after several people asserted I *had to* read <u>Radiant Dawn</u>. I heard Forrest Armstrong read at a convention and his take on cult mentalities gave me The Fear. And I found J. David via an online workshop from the very early years of Bizarro. I remember being pretty rough on him, but I started to follow his work because he clearly had a Voice. And after years of stalking his writing career, I couldn't be more proud to be providing a home for his knockout debut.

On a less side-like and final note—*What's with the ending to this thing?* It's a question I anticipate being asked by about two out of every ten readers. Some people will dig the metaphor. Some people will pick up the (very) subtle clues throughout the narrative. Some people will force their own explanation (see also: most reviews for Mulholland Drive and Donnie Darko). But I think Paul Tremblay is right—even if you're mystified, J. David is spinning the right kind of dark magic, and ultimately his gutsy strangeness is a big part of what makes his brutal mini-epic so unforgettable.

Stay Frosty,

JRJ
Portland, OR 2010

Rbout the Ruthor

James David Osborne lives in Norman, Oklahoma. His work has appeared in The Magazine of Bizarro Fiction, Bare Bone, Verbicide Online, and Bull Spec. His short story "Amends Due, West of Glorieta" was an Honorable Mention for Ellen Datlow's YEAR'S BEST HORROR 2010. He is currently at work on his second novel, a Bizarro noir titled LOW DOWN DEATH RIGHT EASY.

jdavidosborne.tumblr.com

bythetimeweleaveherewellbefriends.blogspot.com

About the Cover Artist

Alex Pardee (born February 5, 1976) is a freelance artist, apparel designer, and writer born in Antioch, California, USA. In addition to having his fine art exhibited in galleries all over the globe, Alex has acted as art director for numerous musical, animated, and film projects. Most notably, for the bands THE USED, IN FLAMES, and hip hop artist CAGE, and for the TV/film projects CHADAM & Zack Snyder's SUCKER PUNCH, for which he created art for the film as well as for the marketing campaign. In 2007, Alex also co-founded a successful art and apparel company called ZEROFRIENDS, which acts as a marketable extension of his artwork and storytelling.

www.zerofriends.com

www.eyesuckink.com

About the Interior Artist

Erin Elise lives in Norman, Oklahoma with her chihuahuas. Occasionally she takes a break from drawing to read, nerd up and dork out, and play with the critters. More art can be found at:

www.facebook.com/erin.elise.art

Bizarro books

CATALOG   SPRING 2010

Bizarro Books publishes under the following imprints:

www.rawdogscreamingpress.com

www.eraserheadpress.com

www.afterbirthbooks.com

www.swallowdownpress.com

For all your Bizarro needs visit:

WWW.BIZARROCENTRAL.COM

Introduce yourselves to the bizarro genre and all of its authors with the Bizarro Starter Kit series. Each volume features short novels and short stories by ten of the leading bizarro authors, designed to give you a perfect sampling of the genre for only $5 plus shipping.

BB-0X1
"The Bizarro Starter Kit"
(Orange)

Featuring D. Harlan Wilson, Carlton Mellick III, Jeremy Robert Johnson, Kevin L Donihe, Gina Ranalli, Andre Duza, Vincent W. Sakowski, Steve Beard, John Edward Lawson, and Bruce Taylor.

236 pages $5

BB-0X2
"The Bizarro Starter Kit"
(Blue)

Featuring Ray Fracalossy, Jeremy C. Shipp, Jordan Krall, Mykle Hansen, Andersen Prunty, Eckhard Gerdes, Bradley Sands, Steve Aylett, Christian TeBordo, and Tony Rauch.

244 pages $5

BB-001"**The Kafka Effekt**" **D. Harlan Wilson** - A collection of forty-four irreal short stories loosely written in the vein of Franz Kafka, with more than a pinch of William S. Burroughs sprinkled on top. **211 pages $14**

BB-002 "**Satan Burger**" **Carlton Mellick III** - The cult novel that put Carlton Mellick III on the map ... Six punks get jobs at a fast food restaurant owned by the devil in a city violently overpopulated by surreal alien cultures. **236 pages $14**

BB-003 "**Some Things Are Better Left Unplugged**" **Vincent Sakwoski** - Join The Man and his Nemesis, the obese tabby, for a nightmare roller coaster ride into this postmodern fantasy. **152 pages $10**

BB-004 "**Shall We Gather At the Garden?**" **Kevin L Donihe** - Donihe's Debut novel. Midgets take over the world, The Church of Lionel Richie vs. The Church of the Byrds, plant porn and more! **244 pages $14**

BB-005 "**Razor Wire Pubic Hair**" **Carlton Mellick III** - A genderless humandildo is purchased by a razor dominatrix and brought into her nightmarish world of bizarre sex and mutilation. **176 pages $11**

BB-006 "**Stranger on the Loose**" **D. Harlan Wilson** - The fiction of Wilson's 2nd collection is planted in the soil of normalcy, but what grows out of that soil is a dark, witty, otherworldly jungle... **228 pages $14**

BB-007 "**The Baby Jesus Butt Plug**" **Carlton Mellick III** - Using clones of the Baby Jesus for anal sex will be the hip sex fetish of the future. **92 pages $10**

BB-008 "**Fishyfleshed**" **Carlton Mellick III** - The world of the past is an illogical flatland lacking in dimension and color, a sick-scape of crispy squid people wandering the desert for no apparent reason. **260 pages $14**

BB-009 **"Dead Bitch Army" Andre Duza** - Step into a world filled with racist teenagers, cannibals, 100 warped Uncle Sams, automobiles with razor-sharp teeth, living graffiti, and a pissed-off zombie bitch out for revenge. **344 pages $16**

BB-010 **"The Menstruating Mall" Carlton Mellick III** - "The Breakfast Club meets Chopping Mall as directed by David Lynch." - Brian Keene **212 pages $12**

BB-011 **"Angel Dust Apocalypse" Jeremy Robert Johnson** - Meth-heads, man-made monsters, and murderous Neo-Nazis. "Seriously amazing short stories..." - Chuck Palahniuk, author of Fight Club **184 pages $11**

BB-012 **"Ocean of Lard" Kevin L Donihe / Carlton Mellick III** - A parody of those old Choose Your Own Adventure kid's books about some very odd pirates sailing on a sea made of animal fat. **176 pages $12**

BB-013 **"Last Burn in Hell" John Edward Lawson** - From his lurid angst-affair with a lesbian music diva to his ascendance as unlikely pop icon the one constant for Kenrick Brimley, official state prison gigolo, is he's got no clue what he's doing. **172 pages $14**

BB-014 **"Tangerinephant" Kevin Dole 2** - TV-obsessed aliens have abducted Michael Tangerinephant in this bizarro combination of science fiction, satire, and surrealism. **164 pages $11**

BB-015 **"Foop!" Chris Genoa** - Strange happenings are going on at Dactyl, Inc, the world's first and only time travel tourism company.

"A surreal pie in the face!" - Christopher Moore **300 pages $14**

BB-016 **"Spider Pie" Alyssa Sturgill** - A one-way trip down a rabbit hole inhabited by sexual deviants and friendly monsters, fairytale beginnings and hideous endings. **104 pages $11**

BB-017 "The Unauthorized Woman" Efrem Emerson - Enter the world of the inner freak, a landscape populated by the pre-dead and morticioners, by cockroaches and 300-lb robots. **104 pages $11**

BB-018 **"Fugue XXIX" Forrest Aguirre** - Tales from the fringe of speculative literary fiction where innovative minds dream up the future's uncharted territories while mining forgotten treasures of the past. **220 pages $16**

BB-019 "Pocket Full of Loose Razorblades" John Edward Lawson - A collection of dark bizarro stories. From a giant rectum to a foot-fungus factory to a girl with a biforked tongue. **190 pages $13**

BB-020 **"Punk Land" Carlton Mellick III** - In the punk version of Heaven, the anarchist utopia is threatened by corporate fascism and only Goblin, Mortician's sperm, and a blue-mohawked female assassin named Shark Girl can stop them. **284 pages $15**

BB-021**"Pseudo-City" D. Harlan Wilson** - Pseudo-City exposes what waits in the bathroom stall, under the manhole cover and in the corporate boardroom, all in a way that can only be described as mind-bogglingly irreal. **220 pages $16**

BB-022 **"Kafka's Uncle and Other Strange Tales" Bruce Taylor** - Anslenot and his giant tarantula (tormentor? fri-end?) wander a desecrated world in this novel and collection of stories from Mr. Magic Realism Himself. **348 pages $17**

BB-023 **"Sex and Death In Television Town" Carlton Mellick III** - In the old west, a gang of hermaphrodite gunslingers take refuge from a demon plague in Telos: a town where its citizens have televisions instead of heads. **184 pages $12**

BB-024 **"It Came From Below The Belt" Bradley Sands** - What can Grover Goldstein do when his severed, sentient penis forces him to return to high school and help it win the presidential election? **204 pages $13**

BB-025 **"Sick: An Anthology of Illness" John Lawson, editor** - These Sick stories are horrendous and hilarious dissections of creative minds on the scalpel's edge. **296 pages $16**

BB-026 **"Tempting Disaster" John Lawson, editor** - A shocking and alluring anthology from the fringe that examines our culture's obsession with taboos. **260 pages $16**

BB-027 **"Siren Promised" Jeremy Robert Johnson & Alan M Clark** - Nominated for the Bram Stoker Award. A potent mix of bad drugs, bad dreams, brutal bad guys, and surreal/incredible art by Alan M. Clark. **190 pages $13**

BB-028 **"Chemical Gardens" Gina Ranalli** - Ro and punk band Green is the Enemy find Kreepkins, a surfer-dude warlock, a vengeful demon, and a Metal Priestess in their way as they try to escape an underground nightmare. **188 pages $13**

BB-029 **"Jesus Freaks" Andre Duza** - For God so loved the world that he gave his only two begotten sons… and a few million zombies. **400 pages $16**

BB-030 **"Grape City" Kevin L. Donihe** - More Donihe-style comedic bizarro about a demon named Charles who is forced to work a minimum wage job on Earth after Hell goes out of business. **108 pages $10**

BB-031 **"Sea of the Patchwork Cats" Carlton Mellick III** - A quiet dreamlike tale set in the ashes of the human race. For Mellick enthusiasts who also adore The Twilight Zone. **112 pages $10**

BB-032 **"Extinction Journals" Jeremy Robert Johnson** - An uncanny voyage across a newly nuclear America where one man must confront the problems associated with loneliness, insane dieties, radiation, love, and an ever-evolving cockroach suit with a mind of its own. **104 pages $10**

BB-033 "Meat Puppet Cabaret" Steve Beard - At last! The secret connection between Jack the Ripper and Princess Diana's death revealed! **240 pages $16 / $30**

BB-034 "The Greatest Fucking Moment in Sports" Kevin L. Donihe - In the tradition of the surreal anti-sitcom Get A Life comes a tale of triumph and agape love from the master of comedic bizarro. **108 pages $10**

BB-035 "The Troublesome Amputee" John Edward Lawson - Disturbing verse from a man who truly believes nothing is sacred and intends to prove it. **104 pages $9**

BB-036 "Deity" Vic Mudd - God (who doesn't like to be called "God") comes down to a typical, suburban, Ohio family for a little vacation—but it doesn't turn out to be as relaxing as He had hoped it would be... **168 pages $12**

BB-037 "The Haunted Vagina" Carlton Mellick III - It's difficult to love a woman whose vagina is a gateway to the world of the dead. **132 pages $10**

BB-038 "Tales from the Vinegar Wasteland" Ray Fracalossy - Witness: a man is slowly losing his face, a neighbor who periodically screams out for no apparent reason, and a house with a room that doesn't actually exist. **240 pages $14**

BB-039 "Suicide Girls in the Afterlife" Gina Ranalli - After Pogue commits suicide, she unexpectedly finds herself an unwilling "guest" at a hotel in the Afterlife, where she meets a group of bizarre characters, including a goth Satan, a hippie Jesus, and an alien-human hybrid. **100 pages $9**

BB-040 "And Your Point Is?" Steve Aylett - In this follow-up to LINT multiple authors provide critical commentary and essays about Jeff Lint's mind-bending literature. **104 pages $11**

BB-041 **"Not Quite One of the Boys" Vincent Sakowski** - While drug-dealer Maxi drinks with Dante in purgatory, God and Satan play a little tri-level chess and do a little bargaining over his business partner, Vinnie, who is still left on earth. **220 pages $14**

BB-042 **"Teeth and Tongue Landscape" Carlton Mellick III** - On a planet made out of meat, a socially-obsessive monophobic man tries to find his place amongst the strange creatures and communities that he comes across. **110 pages $10**

BB-043 **"War Slut"   Carlton Mellick III** - Part "1984," part "Waiting for Godot," and part action horror video game adaptation of John Carpenter's "The Thing." **116 pages $10**

BB-044 **"All Encompassing Trip"   Nicole Del Sesto** - In a world where coffee is no longer available, the only television shows are reality TV re-runs, and the animals are talking back, Nikki, Amber and a singing Coyote in a do-rag are out to restore the light   **308 pages $15**

BB-045 **"Dr. Identity"   D. Harlan Wilson** - Follow the Dystopian Duo on a killing spree of epic proportions through the irreal postcapitalist city of Bliptown where time ticks sideways, artificial Bug-Eyed Monsters punish citizens for consumer-capitalist lethargy, and ultraviolence is essential as a daily multivitamin. **208 pages $15**

BB-046 **"The Million-Year Centipede"   Eckhard Gerdes** - Wakelin, frontman for 'The Hinge,' wrote a poem so prophetic that to ignore it dooms a person to drown in blood. **130 pages $12**

BB-047 **"Sausagey Santa"   Carlton Mellick III** - A bizarro Christmas tale featuring Santa as a piratey mutant with a body made of sausages. 124 pages $10

BB-048 **"Misadventures in a Thumbnail Universe" Vincent Sakowski** - Dive deep into the surreal and satirical realms of neo-classical Blender Fiction, filled with television shoes and flesh-filled skies. **120 pages $10**

BB-049 **"Vacation" Jeremy C. Shipp** - Blueblood Bernard Johnson leaved his boring life behind to go on The Vacation, a year-long corporate sponsored odyssey. But instead of seeing the world, Bernard is captured by terrorists, becomes a key figure in secret drug wars, and, worse, doesn't once miss his secure American Dream. **160 pages $14**

BB-051 **"13 Thorns" Gina Ranalli** - Thirteen tales of twisted, bizarro horror. **240 pages $13**

BB-050 **"Discouraging at Best" John Edward Lawson** - A collection where the absurdity of the mundane expands exponentially creating a tidal wave that sweeps reason away. For those who enjoy satire, bizarro, or a good old-fashioned slap to the senses. **208 pages $15**

BB-052 **"Better Ways of Being Dead" Christian TeBordo** - In this class, the students have to keep one palm down on the table at all times, and listen to lectures about a panda who speaks Chinese. **216 pages $14**

BB-053 **"Ballad of a Slow Poisoner" Andrew Goldfarb** Millford Mutterwurst sat down on a Tuesday to take his afternoon tea, and made the unpleasant discovery that his elbows were becoming flatter. **128 pages $10**

BB-054 **"Wall of Kiss" Gina Ranalli** - A woman... A wall... Sometimes love blooms in the strangest of places. **108 pages $9**

BB-055 **"HELP! A Bear is Eating Me" Mykle Hansen** - The bizarro, heartwarming, magical tale of poor planning, hubris and severe blood loss... **150 pages $11**

BB-056 **"Piecemeal June" Jordan Krall** - A man falls in love with a living sex doll, but with love comes danger when her creator comes after her with crab-squid assassins. **90 pages $9**

BB-057 **"Laredo" Tony Rauch** - Dreamlike, surreal stories by Tony Rauch. **180 pages $12**

BB-058 **"The Overwhelming Urge" Andersen Prunty** - A collection of bizarro tales by Andersen Prunty. **150 pages $11**

BB-059 **"Adolf in Wonderland" Carlton Mellick III** - A dreamlike adventure that takes a young descendant of Adolf Hitler's design and sends him down the rabbit hole into a world of imperfection and disorder. **180 pages $11**

BB-060 **"Super Cell Anemia" Duncan B. Barlow** - "Unrelentingly bizarre and mysterious, unsettling in all the right ways..." - Brian Evenson. **180 pages $12**

BB-061 **"Ultra Fuckers" Carlton Mellick III** - Absurdist suburban horror about a couple who enter an upper middle class gated community but can't find their way out. **108 pages $9**

BB-062 **"House of Houses" Kevin L. Donihe** - An odd man wants to marry his house. Unfortunately, all of the houses in the world collapse at the same time in the Great House Holocaust. Now he must travel to House Heaven to find his departed fiancee. **172 pages $11**

BB-063 **"Necro Sex Machine" Andre Duza** - The Dead Bitch returns in this follow-up to the bizarro zombie epic Dead Bitch Army. **400 pages $16**

BB-064 **"Squid Pulp Blues" Jordan Krall** - In these three bizarro-noir novellas, the reader is thrown into a world of murderers, drugs made from squid parts, deformed gun-toting veterans, and a mischievous apocalyptic donkey. **204 pages $12**

BB-065 "Jack and Mr. Grin" Andersen Prunty - "When Mr. Grin calls you can hear a smile in his voice. Not a warm and friendly smile, but the kind that seizes your spine in fear. You don't need to pay your phone bill to hear it. That smile is in every line of Prunty's prose." - Tom Bradley. **208 pages $12**

BB-066 "Cybernetrix" Carlton Mellick III - What would you do if your normal everyday world was slowly mutating into the video game world from Tron? **212 pages $12**

BB-067 "Lemur" Tom Bradley - Spencer Sproul is a would-be serial-killing bus boy who can't manage to murder, injure, or even scare anybody. However, there are other ways to do damage to far more people and do it legally... **120 pages $12**

BB-068 "Cocoon of Terror" Jason Earls - Decapitated corpses...a sculpture of terror...Zelian's masterpiece, his Cocoon of Terror, will trigger a supernatural disaster for everyone on Earth. **196 pages $14**

BB-069 "Mother Puncher" Gina Ranalli - The world has become tragically over-populated and now the government strongly opposes procreation. Ed is employed by the government as a mother-puncher. He doesn't relish his job, but he knows it has to be done and he knows he's the best one to do it. **120 pages $9**

BB-070 "My Landlady the Lobotomist" Eckhard Gerdes - The brains of past tenants line the shelves of my boarding house, soaking in a mysterious elixir. One more slip-up and the landlady might just add my frontal lobe to her collection. **116 pages $12**

BB-071 "CPR for Dummies" Mickey Z. - This hilarious freakshow at the world's end is the fragmented, sobering debut novel by acclaimed nonfiction author Mickey Z. **216 pages $14**

BB-072 "Zerostrata" Andersen Prunty - Hansel Nothing lives in a tree house, suffers from memory loss, has a very eccentric family, and falls in love with a woman who runs naked through the woods every night. **144 pages $11**

BB-073 **"The Egg Man" Carlton Mellick III** - It is a world where humans reproduce like insects. Children are the property of corporations, and having an enormous ten-foot brain implanted into your skull is a grotesque sexual fetish. Mellick's industrial urban dystopia is one of his darkest and grittiest to date. **184 pages $11**

BB-074 **"Shark Hunting in Paradise Garden" Cameron Pierce** - A group of strange humanoid religious fanatics travel back in time to the Garden of Eden to discover it is invested with hundreds of giant flying maneating sharks. **150 pages $10**

BB-075 **"Apeshit" Carlton Mellick III** - Friday the 13th meets Visitor Q. Six hipster teens go to a cabin in the woods inhabited by a deformed killer. An incredibly fucked-up parody of B-horror movies with a bizarro slant. **192 pages $12**

BB-076 **"Rampaging Fuckers of Everything on the Crazy Shitting Planet of the Vomit At smosphere" Mykle Hansen** - 3 bizarro satires. Monster Cocks, Journey to the Center of Agnes Cuddlebottom, and Crazy Shitting Planet. **228 pages $12**

BB-077 **"The Kissing Bug" Daniel Scott Buck** - In the tradition of Roald Dahl, Tim Burton, and Edward Gorey, comes this bizarro anti-war children's story about a bohemian conenose kissing bug who falls in love with a human woman. **116 pages $10**

BB-078 **"MachoPoni" Lotus Rose** - It's My Little Pony... *Bizarro* style! A long time ago Poniworld was split in two. On one side of the Jagged Line is the Pastel Kingdom, a magical land of music, parties, and positivity. On the other side of the Jagged Line is Dark Kingdom inhabited by an army of undead ponies. **148 pages $11**

BB-079 **"The Faggiest Vampire" Carlton Mellick III** - A Roald Dahlesque children's story about two faggy vampires who partake in a mustache competition to find out which one is truly the faggiest. **104 pages $10**

BB-080 **"Sky Tongues" Gina Ranalli** - The autobiography of Sky Tongues, the biracial hermaphrodite actress with tongues for fingers. Follow her strange life story as she rises from freak to fame. **204 pages $12**

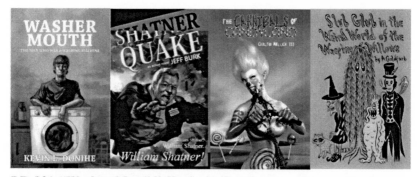

BB-081 **"Washer Mouth" Kevin L. Donihe** - A washing machine becomes human and pursues his dream of meeting his favorite soap opera star. **244 pages $11**

BB-082 **"Shatnerquake" Jeff Burk** - All of the characters ever played by William Shatner are suddenly sucked into our world. Their mission: hunt down and destroy the real William Shatner. **100 pages $10**

BB-083 **"The Cannibals of Candyland" Carlton Mellick III** - There exists a race of cannibals that are made of candy. They live in an underground world made out of candy. One man has dedicated his life to killing them all. **170 pages $11**

BB-084 **"Slub Glub in the Weird World of the Weeping Willows" Andrew Goldfarb** - The charming tale of a blue glob named Slub Glub who helps the weeping willows whose tears are flooding the earth. There are also hyenas, ghosts, and a voodoo priest **100 pages $10**

BB-085 **"Super Fetus" Adam Pepper** - Try to abort this fetus and he'll kick your ass! **104 pages $10**

BB-086 **"Fistful of Feet" Jordan Krall** - A bizarro tribute to spaghetti westerns, featuring Cthulhu-worshipping Indians, a woman with four feet, a crazed gunman who is obsessed with sucking on candy, Syphilis-ridden mutants, sexually transmitted tattoos, and a house devoted to the freakiest fetishes. **228 pages $12**

BB-087 **"Ass Goblins of Auschwitz" Cameron Pierce** - It's Monty Python meets Nazi exploitation in a surreal nightmare as can only be imagined by Bizarro author Cameron Pierce. **104 pages $10**

BB-088 **"Silent Weapons for Quiet Wars" Cody Goodfellow** - "This is high-end psychological surrealist horror meets bottom-feeding low-life crime in a techno-thrilling science fiction world full of Lovecraft and magic..." -John Skipp **212 pages $12**

BB-089 **"Warrior Wolf Women of the Wasteland" Carlton Mellick III**
Road Warrior Werewolves versus McDonaldland Mutants...post-apocalyptic fiction has never been quite like this. **316 pages $13**

BB-090 **"Cursed" Jeremy C Shipp** - The story of a group of characters who believe they are cursed and attempt to figure out who cursed them and why. A tale of stylish absurdism and suspenseful horror. **218 pages $15**

BB-091 **"Super Giant Monster Time" Jeff Burk** - A tribute to choose your own adventures and Godzilla movies. Will you escape the giant monsters that are rampaging the fuck out of your city and shit? Or will you join the mob of alien-controlled punk rockers causing chaos in the streets? What happens next depends on you. **188 pages $12**

BB-092 **"Perfect Union" Cody Goodfellow** - "Croneberg's THE FLY on a grand scale: human/insect gene-spliced body horror, where the human hive politics are as shocking as the gore." -John Skipp. **272 pages $13**

BB-093 **"Sunset with a Beard" Carlton Mellick III** - 14 stories of surreal science fiction. **200 pages $12**

BB-094 **"My Fake War" Andersen Prunty** - The absurd tale of an unlikely soldier forced to fight a war that, quite possibly, does not exist. It's Rambo meets Waiting for Godot in this subversive satire of American values and the scope of the human imagination. **128 pages $11**

BB-095**"Lost in Cat Brain Land" Cameron Pierce** - Sad stories from a surreal world. A fascist mustache, the ghost of Franz Kafka, a desert inside a dead cat. Primordial entities mourn the death of their child. The desperate serve tea to mysterious creatures. A hopeless romantic falls in love with a pterodactyl. And much more. **152 pages $11**

BB-096 **"The Kobold Wizard's Dildo of Enlightenment +2" Carlton Mellick III** - A Dungeons and Dragons parody about a group of people who learn they are only made up characters in an AD&D campaign and must find a way to resist their nerdy teenaged players and retarded dungeon master in order to survive. 232 **pages $12**

ORDER FORM

TITLES	QTY	PRICE	TOTAL

Please make checks and moneyorders payable to ROSE O'KEEFE / BIZARRO BOOKS in U.S. funds only. Please don't send bad checks! Allow 2-6 weeks for delivery. International orders may take longer. If you'd like to pay online via PAYPAL.COM, send payments to publisher@eraserheadpress.com.

SHIPPING: US ORDERS - $2 for the first book, $1 for each additional book. For priority shipping, add an additional $4. INT'L ORDERS - $5 for the first book, $3 for each additional book. Add an additional $5 per book for global priority shipping.

Send payment to:

BIZARRO BOOKS
 C/O Rose O'Keefe
 205 NE Bryant
 Portland, OR 97211

Address		
City	State	Zip
Email	Phone	

CPSIA information can be obtained at www.ICGtesting.com
Printed in the USA
BVOW02s1710120214

344712BV00002B/150/P